Seeing is Believing

Elisa Wilkinson

Fisher King Publishing

Seeing is Believing
Copyright © Elisa Wilkinson 2013
ISBN 978-1-906377-74-8

Fisher King Publishing Ltd
The Studio
Arthington Lane
Pool-in-Wharfedale
LS21 1JZ
England
www.fisherkingpublishing.co.uk

Acknowledgments

I have the privilege to have lived in Wakefield, West Yorkshire, all of my married life and I greatly enjoy this wonderful part of the world.

I am eternally grateful to my husband Eric and my daughter Lesley who have always encouraged me in whatever pursuit I chose to follow, be it researching the paranormal, writing, oil painting or in any other direction I may have been guided to take.

Although we are past retirement age, Eric and I still enjoy our working life; we are self-employed and I help him along with our daughter, to run the numerous businesses that we own, in both America and England.

My good friend Del Iron Cloud, a Native American Indian, who resides in Rapid City, South Dakota, USA, has also been of great support to me for which I give thanks. Anyone who knows him will be aware that he often quotes a saying from the great warrior Lakota Chief, Crazy Horse...

...Never lose faith in what you believe in.

Contents

Preface

Throughout time, ghosts, poltergeists, UFO's and many other inexplicable aspects of phenomena, have held a deep fascination to all mankind. For instance, when a ghost sighting or anything connected to the paranormal occurs, it creates a vast amount of publicity whereupon the curiosity seekers will descend like the plague upon the haunted sight in the hope of witnessing whatever is out there.

I am sorry to say, however, that although each and every one of us is born with a sixth sense, it is more pronounced in some people than others. Therefore, only a privileged few will be capable of seeing or sensing anything out of the ordinary, while the publicity seekers (fakes) will jump on the bandwagon, claiming to see everything and more. These are the people who give genuine psychic investigators a bad name.

A word of warning if you are about to visit a haunted site: never drink alcohol as this blurs the senses! When dealing with the paranormal you need a clear head, for at any moment you may find yourself in a situation that requires a clear and logical mind to deal with the threatening circumstances you may have put yourself in.

When you think that you have seen a ghost you must

always make certain that it is not a figment of your imagination, for the imagination is the biggest trickster of all times.

Taking into consideration your surroundings, anything can trigger an illusion, be it a trick of the light, a flickering candle, the moonlight casting weird shadows as a cloud drifts by, your own hair, or a vehicle's headlights in the fog.

Anything can stimulate a hallucinatory vision, and the imagination will begin working overtime, even more so if you are in a haunted area, where you have heard that more than one person has witnessed the phenomena.

I am often asked, 'How do I find a ghost, and what should I do if I did?'

The answer to that is,' don't worry about it. If there is a ghost about it will make its presence known to you.'

The most well-known factor is by the force causing a sudden change in temperature, where it creates hot and cold spots in rooms or outdoors; draughts sweeping through areas where all windows and doors are tightly secured; unusual sounds and smells; the weird feeling that someone is standing close by, whereupon you feel uneasy and for no apparent reason your flesh is suddenly covered with spine tingling goose bumps; small objects will be moved from their original settings. There are numerous tricks that spirit will play on you, they are, however, usually quite harmless and only wanting to be noticed. 'What do I do if it touches me?' Try not to panic, keep a clear head, and if at all possible ask, 'Who are you and what do you want?' If you are too afraid to speak, then simply ask them to go away by thought.

'What is a ghost?' No one knows for certain, they can only surmise. It can present itself as a person, an animal, an object, even a building, etc. They are most certainly a vision of the past, and can return at will by drawing energy from the person seeing them or from an electrical surge of power, i.e., the television, telephone, generators, pylons, or places where there is a large amount of power being generated. As for buildings, I believe that they are caused by time warps, and only appear for a short while on rare occasions.

It is important not to disturb the recently deceased. When the body dies the soul, for a period of time, goes on to rest. In some cases it cannot as we grieve too heavily for the departed, and can turn to mediums for comfort. By doing so we are not helping the deceased to obtain their well-deserved rest. In fact, we are causing them unnecessary suffering with our inconsiderate actions, as we are constantly pulling at them through these people. Try to imagine that you are exhausted and want to sleep, but just as you are beginning to relax and drift off

Into that wonderful state of deep tranquil peace, you are disturbed by someone calling out your name; bringing you back to full-awareness where there is no way you can get back to sleep again.

Inevitably, this is what happens to the departed when mediums are used. So, leave them alone, they will, if they wish, return when they are ready to. No amount of grieving will help any party. In reality, the grief we are experiencing is for ourselves and not wholly for the deceased, as we are the ones who are left behind. If it is a friend who has died then loved ones would be there to comfort each other. But when it is a husband or wife who is gone, then there is no one to put their arms around us to ease the pain. Or, when we lay alone in our beds at night with no one to cuddle up to, this is when we feel the brunt of our loss, and life doesn't feel worth living any more. Take heart. Just because they are gone from this earthly plane, it does not mean that they have left you entirely. Many of the bereaved have found themselves dreaming about their loved ones, and are told not to worry or fret; they are out of pain now and are happy where they are. Try not to get upset. This is their way of communicating with you, for they know that if they suddenly appeared in the home the shock would be too much for you. So, let them speak in your dreams, it is their way of bringing you comfort and easing the painful separation. Just remember, they are suffering the separation as well as you are. So let them rest, as they are now taking a strange new journey into a different life, and will be preparing for the next one. Therefore, as I have stated earlier, we have to learn how to let go otherwise they will become earthbound.

The shock of unexpected death, be it accidental, road, air, fire or worse, murder, can cause a person to become earthbound. Also, greed, jealousy, hate, fear, revenge, love and cowardice, can create the same effect.

Then there is the person who does not realise that he or she is dead, and are not able to come to terms with their demise, until a medium sees them and informs them that they are dead and must move on to their next lives. Without that knowledge they will continue to haunt that particular area forever. There are also those who fight death to the very end, who do not want to leave this earthly life, and so continue to remain earthbound.

Fear of the material life

Monks and nuns are the most notorious for keeping up a systematic haunting schedule, as they have one of the highest ratings of sightings. They are reputed to stay close to their monastery and convents where they can be seen and heard chanting and praying, as they glide amidst the ruins of ancient buildings. In life they would have felt secure and content in their surroundings, and most likely at their time of passing over they were afraid to face what their next lives would bring, as many entered these places to escape from the realities of material life.

Unnecessary and unexpected death

Victims of road accidents suddenly appear begging lifts from unsuspecting motorists, then disappear while seated in their vehicles, causing a great deal of fear to motorists.

A group of people in the mid 1970's witnessed the re-enactment of the Battle of Marsden Moor. They cowered terrified watching and listening to the screams and groans of the dying men and horses, the clashing of swords and shouts to rally the fighting men, which echoed all around them. In another case, legions of Roman soldiers were seen marching through cellars in York before disappearing through a stone wall.

An American airline pilot, whose Lockheed Tri-Star plane

crashed into the Florida swamps returned to save hundreds of passengers' lives, which would have been lost without his assistance when he informed various crew members about faults on the aircrafts. Upon checking they discovered he was correct.

All of these people have been victims of unnecessary death.

Time slips

We may not realise it, but properties are also living things. They are alive with the energies of every thought, deed and memory of each individual who has lived and died there.

Everywhere is haunted by the past and the present. Leslie and I entered a Tudor building in Cornwall. When we left the impressive building we turned to look at it from across the road and it had disappeared! We called in a local shop and were told that the Tudor building had burnt down in the mid 1950's. A similar mystery happened to a couple who rented a house in France, and were later informed that the house had been demolished years ago.

Lancaster Bombers from the Second World War have suddenly appeared in the sky with their engines reverberating as they roared overhead, and then disappeared as if by magic over various areas of England. Ships at sea have been seen, that have been sunk many years previously. The sights and sounds of skidding and crashing cars and motorbikes haunt our roads.

Every object, be it living or inanimate has, in some incredible way, the amazing ability to reappear whenever it need be. There are so many things in our world that cannot be explained.

Causes of phenomena

An outbreak of phenomena usually occurs with the renovation of an old property or the erection of new buildings on a pre-historic site, or possibly containing a village from the past that has long since been forgotten. Locations I have investigated have been an abandoned quarry that had been filled in and built upon (the drowned girl at Ackworth); a new road or motorway that is under construction (Stocksbridge); and industrial units in Leeds (Tannery Lane ghost). These are some of the recognisable causes for various hauntings mentioned in my book.

Reincarnation and Astral Projection

When the body dies it travels on to its resting place, but what happens when this soul is reincarnated? How do mediums manage to contact these souls after reincarnation?

If the soul has been born into another body, then that soul is experiencing a new lifetime. At times some of us experience a feeling of death or unreality about us, even though we are perfectly healthy. Could this be, that at that precise moment someone is trying to contact our previous personality through a medium, whereby we are left for no apparent reason feeling drained of both physical and mental energy?

We often find that certain individuals have actually altered their appearances to complete strangers, and know nothing about it. One 'normal' housewife was seen for a few moments by two people at the same time as a French Napoleonic soldier, another was seen as a stooping old gypsy, and one as an ancient Egyptian. Think about it, have you ever had to look more than once at a person, the reason being that they looked different at a second and third glance? Are they reincarnates, and are you, for a fleeting second seeing them as they used to be?

In your dreams have you ever lived in a past era? Is this your subconscious mind at work while you sleep, or have you really lived that life before as the dream is so clear and lucid to you? Did you die a normal death in your dreams or was it suicide or murder? So called experts state that when we are running in our dreams we are trying to escape from something that is troubling us. Nonsense, we are reliving some of our past fears from another time and place. The traumatic experiences from which we are running stay with us in each of our lives, until we are cleansed of them through the pathways, to our time of becoming pure energy of light.

Has the strange overwhelming sensation that you are floating or in a semi-comatose condition while you are awake occurred and you think you are daydreaming? Or have you experienced the impression that you are flying through time and space in your sleep? The experience of floating and sensation of flying unaided is meaningful. I believe that when we are asleep our minds are so relaxed that we can enjoy the freedom of release from our bodies and this is when we are astral travelling. People who have undergone this unusual phenomenon have spoken of the wonderful sensation of freedom that they have felt. Some have vivid recollections of their experiences after visiting different parts of the universe, solar systems and planets, travelling through both light and darkness out there in space.

The unbreathable atmosphere of space, under normal conditions, would be suffocating, but, in our astral bodies we can travel anywhere in time and space without issue.

Another form of astral travel that could also be classed as reincarnation is when you drive along a road, and as you turn the corner there stands a building that you immediately recognise, even though you have never been in that vicinity before in your life. Or, when you enter an unfamiliar building and you know exactly what will be on the inside, such as wallpaper, furniture and carpets.

This can also happen with people, when you meet someone who is unknown to you, and for some apparent reason the moment you meet you recognise each other in some way and there is some form of bond between you. What happens? How does this strange phenomenon occur?

It is possible that your astral body has somehow travelled ahead, so you know exactly what is to come, it is quite simple really. Take, for example, my friend who worked in Huddersfield, who saw me appear in her office. At the time I was driving along the Denby Dale road in Wakefield where I saw her hovering above the Asdale roundabout. The very moment we looked at each other we both disappeared.

As I said earlier, every one of us has a sixth sense and the purpose for its existence is for each and every one of us to use it to the best of our ability.

Introduction

There are many questions to be asked regarding the supernatural.

What malevolent force is haunting Pearoyd Bridge and the A161 by-pass at Stocksbridge, where numerous sightings of mysterious apparitions have been witnessed, and many lives have been lost since the road works first began?

Did the children really see the reptilian man enter the wardrobe in their bedroom? If so, was it linked to their father's involvement with UFO's and the Ouija board from the past?

Are people bringing forward demons from another realm with their obsessive behaviour with the Ouija board?

Can dreams predicting the future come true? They did for two ladies. One nearly died of heartbreak, where the other was saved from an evil spirit in a haunted castle dungeon.

Do UFO's exist? Or, are they a figment of our imagination? Hundreds of people living and working in an area sighted a huge craft blotting out half the sky while another two investigators lost three hours of time. Were they abducted by aliens?

Is a battle from the past still raging on the Portobello Estate? Who are the mysterious children?

Why does a walking stick suddenly appear when a man develops gout, then mysteriously disappears when he is recovered?

Why did the boys remain silent for over thirty years and were afraid to speak of an angel sighting in their home town?

There are many more factual happenings in this book that I am certain that readers will find of particular interest. I have given a full detailed account of what each person had experienced. I personally believe that all hauntings; poltergeist, ghosts, angels, UFO's etc, are all a natural phenomenon that have been with us throughout time. In this book I have tried to give a reasonable and logical explanation for all the reported events.

The Chantry Bridge Phantom

Thursday evening, November 1988, was dull and drizzling with rain as John Lambing drove his wife Debra home, travelling from Wakefield towards Doncaster Road. Debra had been day dreaming as she stared ahead at the slow moving traffic, but suddenly became alert as they crossed the new Chantry Bridge, where she observed an ominous figure standing in the rain swept darkness near the parapet of the old Chantry Bridge.

At that moment the traffic lights changed to red and John brought the car to a halt practically parallel to the figure. Debra nudged her husband saying, "John, look at that strange man, what do you think he's doing?"

He looked over to where she was indicating and saw what appeared to be a man dressed in a long black cloak with a pointed hood. Only part of his face was visible as he was staring down into the water below, but what he could see of him was frightening, for it bore a strange unearthly bluish glow.

"You don't think he's going to jump in the river, do you?" Debra asked.

"I don't know," John replied, "but it does look a bit odd to me."

The tooting of impatient drivers made him realise the traffic lights had changed and he had to move.

"Quick, get into the other lane and turn around at the lights so we can have another look, Debra said excitedly.

John swung the car over into the third lane to the next set of lights and drove back up Kirkgate to the roundabout, so that they could return over the bridge and position themselves better to see what it was.

As the old bridge came into view Debra gasped, "it's still there. I didn't think it would be." The phantom had apparently known what they would do, and was awaiting their return, for, as John drove steadily over the new bridge and stopped where both bridges met, with a fast gliding motion the phantom swept across the old bridge towards them and stopped within a range of fifteen feet. By this time Debra had the car window wide open so that they could see the phantom figure clearly. At first it held its head down, but as soon as they both began to look at it, simultaneously it lifted its head and looked directly at them, revealing the ghastliest sight they had ever encountered.

"Good god, look at its face," John croaked, "what the hell is it?" Debra was too shocked to say anything as they stared in horror at the polished bone of a shining white skull illuminated eerily in the brilliant glare of the street lights. The couple felt as invisible penetrating eyes were watching them through the black empty eye sockets transfixed upon them, and in their fear were being laughed at by the hideous grinning mouth. At the same time the gruesome spectre was gliding towards them and they couldn't move a muscle. They just sat transfixed by the appalling sight. Then, as it was almost upon them it vanished. At that moment the hypnotic spell was broken, and traffic lights at red or not John drove through them to the safety of his home.

Other witnesses have come forward to say that they have also seen the same apparition on the old bridge, including a bus driver, as they were crossing onto the new bridge. It has been recorded that during the War of the Roses in 1461 the third son of the Duke of York, Edmund, was killed on the bridge by Lord Clifford. Perhaps it is his ghost, or, it may be a monk who worked in the Chantry Chapel on the bridge. Who knows? Maybe, if you are brave enough, you could go out there one dark and stormy night and try to find out for yourselves!

The Floating Highwayman

If you were to travel about four miles out of Wakefield on Denby Dale Road you would see to the left of you, at Blacker Lane crossroads, a pub named The British Royal Oak, which was originally an old coaching house. Just a few yards further Branch Road leads to Bretton Hall, built in 1720 for Sir William Wentworth. Extremely lavish parties were held at the Hall, and were attended by people trying to outshine each other with their fashionable furs, clothes and jewellery. Therefore, as they travelled to the Hall they would have been easy prey for the local highwaymen who roamed the dark and lonely roads in those times.

Branch Road is the most likely place, that when any of the highwaymen were caught, they would have been hung on the gibbet there and left to rot as a caution to other robbers. Nonetheless, it was here at Branch Road that Dennis Hill was to slip back in time for a few short moments when he saw a gruesome apparition floating before him.

Mid-May brought about a wonderfully clear night. The moon glowed with a fluorescent blue-white clearness, lighting everything beneath it. The stars twinkled brightly from a cloudless sky, bringing about a wonderful feeling of peacefulness and tranquillity. The trees and grass were still and a strange eeriness settled in the surrounding countryside. The only sound to disturb the silence was the engine of an approaching motor car that steadily made its way along the narrow winding road.

Inside the car Dennis Hill, a happy, home-loving man, was blissfully unaware of what was about to happen to him.

As he drove down Branch Road he was thinking of how much he had enjoyed himself at the bowling club. His team had won the match! He glanced at the clock on the dashboard and saw it was 10.15pm. He had just driven round a bend and was on the final stretch of Branch Road before coming onto Denby Dale Road, when unexpectedly he saw, hovering in the field before him, the dark silhouette of a man. Slowing his car down to a crawling pace, Dennis stared in disbelief at what he was witnessing, and shuddered at the morbid sight as he drew alongside of him. "Good grief, I don't believe it," he said aloud. The man was suspended in mid-air, about seven or eight feet from the ground, his head lolled grotesquely to one side, his neck had been broken. Dennis looked above the man's head expecting to see a tree branch, or something that he could have been suspended from, but there was nothing, not even a rope, but there was one thing of which he was certain, the man had been hanged.

Although deeply shocked at the macabre sight that he was witnessing, Dennis stopped the car. Taking great care, he avoided looking at the man's ghastly features and forced himself to concentrate on what he was wearing. He was dressed entirely in black, and had on a long frock coat made of thick, heavy material that was fitted at the waist then flared out at the bottom. The cuffs of the sleeves were cut in a castellation style, and they too looked very thick and heavy. The coat was buttoned pretty high up so he could not see any shirt or waistcoat. On his feet he wore a pair of black boots that, he presumed came up to his knees, but he could not say for certain as the coat was so long. His hair was drawn loosely back from his face and tied at the nape of his neck.

Dennis took in as much detail as he could, before the sinister aspect of the situation began to dawn on him. He was alone on the road with no one else about apart from a floating corpse! It was then that he leapt back inside his car, put it into gear and accelerated away from that lonely place. Although he felt as if he should have gone back to take another look, his courage failed him. He had seen enough. He has driven along the same road on many occasions since that night, but he has never witnessed anything there again.

Something Cold Touched Me

When something gently touched her shoulder in the early hours of the morning, Anne Harrison fully expected to find her six year old daughter Claire, standing beside her bed.

Yet, when she turned over and switched on the light, no one was there. 'That's odd,' she thought, 'I could have sworn someone touched me, in fact, I know they did.' She sat bolt upright in bed. Concerned, but not afraid, she glanced about the room, then turned her attention to her daughter's bedroom, directly across the landing. She could see quite clearly as they always left both bedroom doors open, that Claire was sound asleep.

"I wonder what it was?" she muttered, and woke her husband, Clive to tell him what had happened. His sleepy useless response was, "it must have been the plant, go back to sleep." He turned over and began snoring.

"Typical," she grumbled, as she switched off the light and slid beneath the bedcovers.

The following morning at breakfast Anne approached the subject of the previous night's incident, but Clive passed it off as imagination. A few nights later, however, he was to be proved wrong.

It was well after midnight, when, for some unknown

reason Anne was jolted wide awake, and her attention drawn to her daughter's bedroom, where she saw in the semi-darkness, a glowing ominous figure draped in white standing beside Claire's bed, looking down at the sleeping child.

"Oh, my god," she cried, as she pulled herself upright, and then froze as the phantom turned in a slow tormenting manner towards her. Her hair practically stood on end when she found herself facing a spine chilling spectre, a spectre with no face.

Icy tendrils of fear gripped her insides as the phantom began to glide in a slow steady motion towards her, causing her throat to constrict and become dry and parched as terror abounded throughout her. As it drew closer she could see, protruding beneath its hooded head, an awesome grinning skull, from where hollow black eye sockets of indiscernible depth appeared to penetrate her brain, trapping her in a callous, paralysing grip of unimaginable horror. Unable to move or utter a sound, Anne stared boggle eyed and helpless at the daunting creature. Then, without warning and as quick as a flash it was gone.

At that precise moment Anne found herself free from the invisible force that had enveloped her and let out an almighty scream.

"Clive! Clive! Wake up," she yelled, grabbing his arm and shoulder and shaking him.

"What's wrong now?" he snapped. He pulled himself upright and tried to comprehend what Anne was saying. "What is it? Why are you shouting?"

His attitude soon changed when Anne told him what had happened. Without a moment's hesitation Anne and Clive rushed over to their daughter's bedside, concerned at what Anne had seen and heard. But they need not have worried for the little girl was fast asleep, totally oblivious to what her mother had seen.

They couldn't sleep for the rest of that night, and the following day both agreed that nothing must be said in front of Claire, and tried to carry on as normal. Nevertheless, they began a rota of trying to stay awake and watch for the phantom's return. Clive was scared stiff.

As the nights passed by nothing out of the ordinary occurred and they began to relax their vigilance, when Anne did something that she had never done before, and closed both bedroom doors, shutting off sight of their daughter. Although Clive thought this rather unusual he didn't say anything in case it upset her, as both were suffering from stress, and their nerves were jangled at the time.

Regardless of this, whatever was haunting them must have felt the closed doors were a challenge. Clive woke up in the early hours of the morning to the sound of footsteps clomping up and down the staircase, and after sitting and looking around the bedroom was staggered to find both bedroom doors wide open. Amidst the entire racket going on he was further surprised to see both his wife and daughter fast asleep oblivious to all the commotion on the stairs.

Despite the sense of foreboding threatening to encompass him, Clive rose from the bed taking care not to waken his wife and made his way over to the landing where he felt himself walking into an unnatural freezing cold domain between both bedrooms.

Even after he had pressed the switch, bathing the staircase in a brilliant glow of light, the invisible intruder continued its race pounding as loudly as possible both up and down the staircase, regardless of Clive's presence. In the end he gave up, there was nothing he could do so he switched off the light and went back to bed, where he lay unable to sleep, terrified and frozen.

The following day he told Anne, and was astounded when she said she had heard nothing unusual, but did ask why he hadn't woken her. He replied, "because I didn't want to scare you."

However, a few days later the phenomenon occurred throughout the day. This time it was while Claire was playing in her bedroom. Her parents were alerted by her screams, as she raced down stairs crying that something cold had touched her and then moved her drawings. "Look after her, and stay in this room," Clive ordered, closing the lounge door, then bounded upstairs into her bedroom but was stopped short as an intense freezing cold atmosphere engulfed him.

"This is ridiculous," he said, rubbing his arms and looking around the room. "It's freezing in here. I can understand why she came down in such a state." From where he stood he could see where Claire had been drawing as her coloured pencils and paper were scattered in a heap on top of other things over at the other side of the room. Shaking his head, unable to comprehend what was happening to them he returned to the lounge.

A few nights later however, they were surprised around midnight when Claire came downstairs into the lounge and asked why they had pulled back her bedcovers and shaken her awake, then left her?

Clive said she must have been dreaming, but the child had not missed the look of fear that had passed between her parents and refused to return to bed and began to cry. The only way to calm her was to allow her to drop to sleep on the settee until they retired to bed. Most nights Claire would go to bed on her own and sleep through until the following day, but on the odd occasion she would come downstairs crying refusing to go to sleep in her own room. When questioned by her parents asking what was wrong, she would say, "something cold keeps touching me, and you don't believe me." The only way to pacify her was to allow her to drop off to sleep with them before returning her to her own bedroom.

Things, however, came to a head one night when they were awoken by a tremendous crash emanating from the child's bedroom, followed by Claire's agonising screams of terror. Upon entering her bedroom they found her bicycle, that had placed upside down awaiting a new wheel, had been forcibly lifted and thrown over to the other side of the room, and was now on top of the wardrobe, completely out of the reach of Claire. There was no possible way that the little girl could have placed the bicycle where it was found. All three of them spent the rest of the night huddled together in one bed afraid to turn off the light or go to sleep.

Throughout the next few weeks peculiar things occurred that set their nerves on edge, and they decided to bring in the clergy. Yet, even after the vicar had blessed the house nothing changed, and in the end they were forced to move out.

In 1991 Clive rented the property out, but he could never get any of the tenants to stay very long. The reason they gave was that something would sit on the bed at night and pull back the bedcovers. Other tenants complained of something cold touching them and shaking their shoulders. In any event he could not get anyone to stay there for very long.

Although the property is now empty and locked up, when he has called to check on his house, neighbours have told him they can hear someone moving about inside, and in the early hours of the morning are disturbed by someone racing up and down the staircase. Sadly, his marriage broke up a short while later, and Clive found himself staying in his old terrace house.

While lying in bed one hot summer night, he felt the temperature of the room begin to drop rapidly. At first he put it down to the night drawing to a close, however, when a swift freezing cold wind began to blow about the bedroom when all the doors and windows in the house were closed, he panicked, leapt from the bed, grabbed his clothes and spent the rest of the night at his ex-wife's house.

He has never dared to stay another night in that house, nor will he ever enter it alone. As he told me of the happenings his arms were covered in goose pimples. It has frightened him and ruined his family life.

Witchcraft Curses and Ghosts

I find a genuine account of witchcraft and ghosts such a delightful combination of mystery and intrigue that they border beyond all realms of the imagination. So much so, they invoke a thorough in-depth investigation into every aspect of what has been written and spoken of the people involved. From visiting the Kings Arms public house one night in the early 1970's, where I and another lady, a complete stranger to me, saw two apparitions.

To the present day in 1997, where after finding an old tape recording of Heath Old Hall, I began a full investigation into that rare sighting. An incident so rare that it eventually led me into a vale of metaphysical treachery between the entwining strange lives of Lady Mary Bolles of Heath Old Hall, and Mary Pannall, the local witch of her time in the mid 1500's.

The Kings Arms, Heath Common, Wakefield

The Kings Arms has kept its unique character by retaining the original features of dark oak panelling and stone flagged floor that line the narrow, gas-lit passages, prior to winding past two small antiquated rooms before entering the main bar, wherein you will find a pair of nondescript inglenook fireplaces containing huge cast iron firedogs and grates.

Above these are the Kings Arms own Coat of Arms carved in the old panelling that surrounds the entire room and bar. Hanging from the ceiling and protruding from each wall are the old fashioned gas lights. These really enhance the pub's character and on a cold winter night when the log fires are crackling in the grates, spurting out red tongues of flame and casting eerie shadows in the room's gloomy atmosphere, you may find yourself slipping back in time and experiencing a part of the past tragic history where the building now stands.

It was here that Queen Margaret, daughter of the Duke of Anjou and Maine, who wed Henry VI in 1444, was camped during her involvement in the bloody War of the Roses. It was on such a cold blustery night that Lind Daleman and I decided to have a drink there. We had been talking for most of the night, and then settled back to relax and enjoy our drinks by the warmth of the fireside. By and by the crowd began to diminish and the bar was practically empty, apart from two more couples, when something strange happened.

A pale grey mist evolved from the far corner of the bar. From the mist emerged a young girl, aged between fourteen to sixteen years, struggling to carry pewter tankards and earthenware jugs on what appeared to be a wooden tray. She wore a drab tattered skirt that came to her ankles, which was partially covered by a grubby stained white apron. On her head she had a white mop cap that covered her long straggling hair which hung about her shoulders in an unkempt manner; her feet were bare and dirty. Hanging onto her skirt was a little girl aged about seven years old, who was also dressed in a similar manner.

As the poor wretched girl struggled beneath the cumbersome weight my heart went out to her, and at that precise moment our eyes met. She said her name was Mary and the child, Fern. They then both vanished. Within seconds of their de-materializing I glanced at Linda, who seemed oblivious to the young ghosts. However, when I looked across at the young couple opposite the woman's face was ashen. "Did you see that?" I asked. She picked up her bag and jumped to her feet, saying, "I did, but I don't want to talk about it." She fled from the room, followed by her anxious husband asking what was wrong. Linda never saw a thing. The only thing she noticed was the sharp drop in temperature!

That night, as I lay in bed, I found it difficult to sleep as the memory of what I had seen filled my mind. I decided to return the following day. When I did return to the Kings Arms and asked if any of the staff or customers had experienced anything out of the ordinary, the looks on their faces said it all. However, no one was willing to discuss the matter, apart from one of the waitresses who said they would lose their jobs if they said anything to anybody, due to the fact that the person in charge was afraid of ghosts and it would be bad for business, so I thanked them and left.

Outside of the pub I looked with interest at the hexagram window, which is at the front of the building. An elderly gentleman saw me and informed me that Heath Old Hall and the surrounding area had once housed the Templar Movement. This is shown carved into the shields over the fireplaces in the Kings Arms and also Heath Old Hall. He also told me that the pub was haunted by a serving girl and a child.

They had been seen by both customers and staff, some of who had left their jobs because they were afraid. He also pointed out that there was an old Gothic church with unusual graves just beyond the village that may be of interest to me.

I decided to visit the old church, when, after driving a short distance along the narrow twisting roads I came to a hill where something strange happened. In the dip of the hill four horse riders were crossing the road when the spectral figure of Mary appeared in its centre, sending the horses into an uncontrollable frenzy. Two of the riders had to fight to restrain the terrified animals as they raced out of control, bucking and whinnying onto nearby farmland, while the others reared and kicked at the sight of the apparition.

By now I had stopped my car and watched from a good distance away, so that my car would not be damaged or blamed for their peculiar antics, and waited for them to clear the road before proceeding down the hill to the cemetery where I received another unexpected sighting. Upon getting out of the car she materialized again, this time in the cemetery opposite the church.

Without hesitation I ran towards her and followed as she floated just a few yards towards the hedge. Where she stopped and pointed to the ground before fading away. Upon reaching the place where she had been pointing there was nothing to see, no grave stone, or mound of earth or sunken area to provide me with a clue as to what she was trying to show me. The only answer I could surmise was that she must have committed suicide and was buried on unconsecrated ground.

At that time witchcraft had never entered my mind. After

leaving the cemetery and driving home I rang Linda asking if she would like to go to the churchyard with me to see if we could find anything unusual. She agreed and we made arrangements for me to pick her up the following Saturday night. By 11.00pm on the appointed date we had arrived at our destination and had parked the car facing a homeward direction, leaving it with the headlights on, and had a torch each as it was extremely dark out there.

We were disappointed to find both the churchyard and graveyard gates opposite were hung with heavy chains and padlocks. Regardless of this, I said to Linda, "This isn't going to put me off," and handed her my torch leaving my hands free to climb over the graveyard gate.

I had no sooner placed my foot on the lower bar and was about to climb over, when we heard footsteps approaching. We turned and listened as the sound grew closer and closer then passed us by, echoing off into the far distance. The footsteps were definitely male, and by all reasonable accounts were so close we should have seen somebody yet no one was there. That was when Linda suggested that it might be a good idea to climb over the churchyard gate instead.

I jumped down and followed her across the road, where, after wondering how to get over this set of gates, I gave the torch to Linda and told her to shine it where I could see what I was doing. I managed to reach the top when the light began to move about in a jerky manner. "Linda, hold the light still. I can't see what I'm doing," I whispered sharply. "It isn't me," she replied, "if you look, my light is on your hands." Something happened then that made me forget about the height of the gate and I reached the ground in record time, when I saw my Jaguar car that I had parked twenty feet away, was bouncing up and down like a yo-yo. My first thought was that somebody was playing about, and I ran to the bouncing vehicle fully expecting to see someone there, but there was no-one.

The phenomenon was far from over because while we were standing on the pavement watching the car a weird blue glow began to emanate from the stone wall beside us causing us to take a few steps backwards.

We watched in fascination, when the spectral figure of what appeared to be a short thin woman draped in a faded pale blue grey cowled robe floated out through the graveyard wall, and hovered just a few feet away from us. The incredible sensation of such a rare sighting practically overwhelmed me, to be so close to such an amazing phenomenon was staggering. Nevertheless, I did change my mind when the wraith lifted its head and looked straight at us. For as long as I live I will never forget staring into the emptiness of two depressed black hollows set in the aged yellow bone of a gruesome skull. That did it, enough was enough. I ran to the driver's door and unlocked it shouting for Linda to get into the car. She didn't need telling a second time and leapt in.

Regardless of my getaway speed the ghastly spectre had partially materialized into the rear of the car. Poor Linda was terrified and could not stop screaming. However, when we passed Heath Old Hall it disappeared. All the incidents of the night had been too much for Linda, who had never experienced any kind of phenomena before. When we arrived at her home she jumped out of the car and raced into the house, then reappeared with her mother, who began throwing Holy Water both inside and outside the car whilst praying. In spite of all their prayers and sprinkling of Holy Water, it did no good, for when I arrived home the spectre appeared on the landing and was looking out towards Sandal Castle. It took three mediums and myself nearly three weeks to rid our home of the ghastly apparition. This brings me to the present time and date.

In late August 1997 I was looking through some old television news tape recordings, that I had made many years previously, and by chance I happened to come across one of Lady Mary Bolles, who had been seen by various people, haunting the ruins of Heath Old Hall, situated on Heath Common near Wakefield. It was also stated that her father, Squire Witham from Ledsham near Castleford, had been cursed by a witch named Mary Pannall. As I watched this piece of news, submerged memories began to awaken in my mind, bringing forward the unforgettable weird phenomena that Linda and I had experienced some years later at Kirkthorpe churchyard. A number of years after our encounter I had found out that Lady Mary haunted the churchyard, and it was highly probable that it was her we had seen. If not, then it could have been one of the eight nuns, who for some strange reason, are buried at Kirkthorpe churchyard.

The nuns were from a French Benedictine Order, who had taken over the Old Hall after they came to England to escape their own country's revolution. They had left France on

October 18th 1792 and settled at the Old Hall, where they remained until 1821. The Abbess was Madame Louise Levis de Montargis le Mirepoix. She ruled over forty to forty two nuns, besides novices, pupils, servants and outdoor employees, the latter totalling about eighty people.

In a bid to discover who was haunting the churchyard I drove to the village of Ledsham, where, from speaking to the locals and studying written historical accounts of the Witham

Lady Mary Bolles began her life in 1578 as Mary Witham, daughter of Squire Witham, the wealthy land owner of who it is recorded that the estate of Ledstone and the patronage of Ledsham church, was either sold or granted by King Edward VI to his father Henry Witham, who died in 1572.

The estate, then being handed down to his son, William Witham, Lady Mary's father. Her first husband was Thomas Jobson (Jopson) esquire, of Cudworth, Royston, Yorkshire, by whom she bore two children, Thomas and Elizabeth.

After his death, she married Thomas Bolles (Bowles) of Osberton, Nottinghamshire, by whom she had two more daughters, Anne and Mary. When Thomas Bolles died on 19th March 1653, King Charles granted the rare title of Baronetcy of Nova Scotia to Lady Dame Mary Bolles and to her heirs whatever. Lady Mary spent most of her life at the Heath Old Hall at the top of the common, where the family owned most of the land and property situated there. It is also recorded that she entertained in lavish style and exhibited a great deal of eccentricity throughout her life. Also, that her failure to carry out the elaborate instructions in the will maybe one of the causes for her haunting there. On the other hand it might be an overwhelming burden of conscience, knowing that in some way she was responsible for an innocent woman's death.

The woman in question was Mary Pannall, the local witch. It is believed that throughout her younger years Lady Mary was an active member of Mary Pannall's coven, and was deeply involved in the act of witchcraft and the black arts. If this is so, then Mary Pannall might not have been of such low breeding, or the wandering rouge some would like us to think she was. Perhaps her family had at some time belonged to the gentry.

The whole scenario would then take on a different aspect. She must have had some form of respect in the community for her to have been involved with Lady Mary's friends and family, or they would have driven her out of the area. It is common sense that Lady Mary would not have become involved with the coven at such an early age unless she had been introduced by someone of a higher status. It is by far more of a coincidence that Lady Mary was initiated into the coven when she became fourteen years old, the age of puberty. At the same time, Squire Witham died, as the writings state, 'by Witchcraft.'

It appears that more than one member in that family was also involved in the craft, otherwise she would not have been accepted, for a genuine dedicated coven is an extremely hard order to join, as it commands servitude, loyalty and secrecy from everyone involved. Only selected individuals were permitted to join.

Something else that is strange and requires consideration is that Mary Pannall cursed Squire Witham and caused his death by uttering the words,

'None of ye shall rest until I have had my revenge.' Those words were not valid enough reason to have an innocent woman executed. There must have been a much deeper involvement between the Squire and Mary Pannall as to what is written, for uttering those words did not deem the death penalty, even in those days. A more logical explanation would be that perhaps Mary Pannall was killed because she held an extremely powerful hold over her ladyship. Maybe she was silenced because she knew too much about the family and community, where she was feared by all. This would account for the horrific, unnecessary death of Mary Pannall, who was incarcerated in York Castle, where she was found guilty of witchcraft in 1603. The charge made was for causing the death of Squire Witham.

Another strange fact is that at the time of Mary Pannall's execution, Lady Mary would have been twenty four. Ten years had lapsed since she had uttered those fateful words.

After her totally ludicrous trial ten years later, Mary was taken from York Castle to the crossroads at Kippax, where a crude gallows had been built, and from a horse drawn cart on which she stood, a coarse rope shaped into a noose was pulled over her head and tightened around her neck, before the horse was led away, leaving Mary Pannall to die in the most horrendous manner of strangulation. Her body was left to rot as a warning to all who were involved with the craft.

If Lady Mary and other members of the coven had attended the barbaric execution then Mary Pannall would have recognised many faces there and wondered why no one had spoken out in her favour. Her anger at them would undoubtedly have been at its uttermost, for she would have felt betrayed by all who had turned out for this public mockery of justice. As for in her final agonising moments of life, I would look more to the curse, 'None of ye shall rest until I have my revenge,' being cast directly at them, especially Lady Mary and not at her father.

It is little wonder that she cursed the whole Witham line. Lady Mary had betrayed her mentor and had been cursed. Her haunting of Ledsham church, its grounds and Heath Old Hall every 9th May, and also in its ruins along the old coach road could be explained as conscience.

The curse and her guilt would not allow her to rest. Because of the cruel injustice done to Mary Pannall, the old roman road named Ridge Road, where she was hung, was renamed Mary Pannall Road in her memory. She was the last person to be hung as a witch in Yorkshire.

With regard to Mary Bolles and her will; there was something very peculiar about her last request, and that was for her bowels to be removed and buried elsewhere in a secret location. Perhaps she was trying to defy the curse, who knows? There was one thing; however, whatever she was trying didn't work! She has not found peace. In years gone by, it was quite commonplace to remove the vital organs from the body, including the bowels of a witch, for it is said that a witch cannot return unless she is complete. Lady Mary also ordered that her body was to remain in her room at her home for six weeks after her death, and to provide that money should be available 'to retain her kindred friends to entertain other persons ordinary and EXTRAORDINARY!'

The Kirkthorpe church register says; 'The bowels of Dame Mary Bolles of Heath was buried on the 5th day of May in the churchyard of Kirkythorpe.'

In the ancient church at Ledsham you will find that the tomb of Lady Mary, that once stood within railings, close to the communion table, has now been moved to the northern corner facing away from the congregation and altar. It is written that her tomb was moved to the far corner to allow more space in the church. Others believe that this was done because of her involvement with the black arts, and did not want a life size effigy facing the congregation.

There are no longer any railings around her tomb, which, incidentally, seems to have been re-built in a slipshod manner. Maybe she knew this was going to happen, for when her tomb was disturbed and the masons were in the act of moving it the church doors opened unexpectedly, followed by a heavy gust of wind that blew dust around the church before all was still again. It appears that Mary Pannall has had her revenge, but she paid the ultimate price with her life.

The tomb of Lady Mary in the north-facing
corner of Ledsham Church

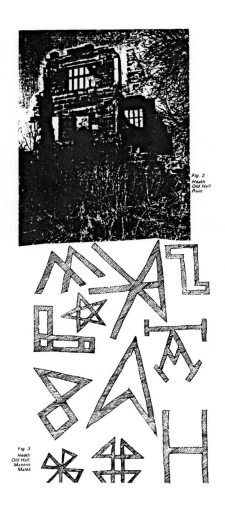

Fig. 2
Heath
Old Hall
Ruin

Fig 3
Heath
Old Hall.
Masons
Marks

Heath, Muir & Mary Addie at Heath in Yorkshire

Haunted Cottages at Ledsham

Situated to the rear of Ledsham church stands a row of old stone cottages, that in the past were actually hospital cottages built for the local people in 1670 by Sir John Lewis. In 1959 the cottages were modernised and re-named Sir John's Cottages. These old buildings have been prone to various types of phenomena.

Mrs Joyce Hurst and her husband, who reside in one of the cottages told me, "On the first night we moved in a strange thing occurred." As they laid in bed a loud whooshing sound could be heard building up in the wall. Laying absolutely still, not daring to move, they listened as the sound continued to intensify, before finally breaking free and rushing through the bedroom at an incredible speed then disappeared through the curtains and closed window. Joyce stated, "There was no wind that night, and the window was definitely closed. It was impossible for any draught of such velocity to blow through an enclosed room. It just sounded like a gale force wind blowing past us."

In 1995 Margaret Helmsley, who lives at number three declared that 'she had just dropped off to sleep, when for no apparent reason she was jolted wide awake and saw to her surprise an elderly lady seated in the chair opposite with her arms folded looking extremely contented as she gazed into the fire. The lady's grey hair was drawn to the back of her head, making her sharp pointed features stand out clearly against the chair's headrest. Margaret also noticed that she wore a rough looking shawl around her shoulders and a long dress. She appeared to be very poor. After staying for a few moments she disappeared.

Alan and Joan Johnson, who used to live at number five, often used to get the smell of tobacco smoke in various rooms of the house that would linger for a while and then go away. They later found out that the man who had died there used to be an ardent pipe smoker.

Mr Arthur Langdale from number eleven saw an old lady dressed in black clothing edged with white, wearing a mop cap on her head, suddenly appear in his bedroom. She then proceeded to walk straight through the fitted wardrobe. The area in which she appeared was where the original stone staircase had been. Situated on top of a cabinet in his lounge are two framed photographs, one of his mother and the other his daughter. He places the photographs facing forward, but when he looks at them he finds they have been turned inwards facing each other. This is a regular occurrence. One day whilst he was seated in the lounge relaxing, for no apparent reason a large ornamental horse that he keeps on top of the cabinet fell onto the floor and smashed into minute pieces. It was beyond repair.

He also has another problem; at times he cannot find what he is searching for. The reason is that certain objects have been moved from their original position and are found to have been placed in other rooms of his home. He says, "It doesn't bother me anymore, I'm used to it."

Sometime later, Joan and Alan moved to number seven, and Joan, who was a qualified nurse before her retirement, used to take care of her neighbour at number ten who had cancer. She often called throughout the day to check that Vera was alright. However, as Vera's condition deteriorated she became bedridden, and her daughter, who lived at Pontefract, took her to stay at her home. Joan would often travel to Pontefract and sit with her old friend throughout the night.

As the weeks passed by Joan became very tired and told Vera that she had arranged for a nurse to come and sit with her, just for one night, as she needed to catch up on her sleep. The well-deserved rest was to be denied her, for in the early hours of the morning Alan and Joan were woken by the sound of an alarm system close by. They leapt out of bed, pulled on their slippers and dressing gowns and hurried outside to see which one of the tenants alarms had been activated, and were surprised to find it was their own.

The other tenants, who were by now gathered outside, asked what was wrong. They were as baffled as their neighbours and apologised, telling everyone to return to their beds and they would silence the alarm. However, after numerous attempts they could not turn it off, and in the end two of the men got a ladder, climbed up and switched off the whole lot. All the cottages have a connecting system and a light flashes outside whichever cottage is in need of help, so it was essential to get an electrician out to fix the problem as soon as possible. But, after checking the system he could find nothing wrong with it.

Later that day Joan rang Vera's daughter and was told that Vera had been very restless the night before and crying, I don't want a nurse, I want Joan." Vera had passed away in the early hours of the morning. When Joan asked "Was it between 2.00 and 2.30am that Vera had died?"

The daughter replied, "Why, yes, how did you know?" Joan then told her about the early morning events, believing that the alarm system going off in her cottage was Vera's way of trying to contact her. She stated, "It was a weird experience. I had never been one to believe in anything like that, but Vera had got through to me in the only way she knew how."

The Phantom Horse
Doncaster Road, Wakefield

The first sign that something mysterious was about to happen to Bill and Josey Brown began as they travelled one evening along Doncaster Road towards Wakefield. Twilight dusk was beginning to fall and the light evening mist cast an eerie glow through the car's headlights. As Bill drove along he mentioned to his wife that the traffic was unusually light on that stretch of road for the time of evening and she agreed.

They had just driven along past the Crofton Arms public house that was to their right when suddenly tiny clouds of mist began to swirl and twist about the car making odd sporadic intermittent movements, before dissolving into nothing. Thinking it a little unusual, Bill didn't say anything and carried on driving, but, as he approached the railway bridge, just before Redbeck Café, he slammed his foot on the brake. A strapping shire-horse, hauling a huge, old fashioned high sided cart, suspended on two big wheels, pulled out from the side of the bridge, crossed the road and disappeared as it reached the pavement edge. They could clearly see that the driver wore a flat cap, his shirt sleeves rolled up and his trousers tied around his ankles with a piece of string. The pair sat opened mouth and gaped at what they had seen, before

Bill, who has always been a sceptic of the paranormal, turned to his wife and stammered, "I've just seen a horse and cart cross the road." "My god," she replied, "you're not the only one, so have I."

There was no way any conventional horse and cart could have driven from that area of field as it was on a completely different level to the road and lay of the land. Both agreed on what they had seen, right down to the last detail of the driver on the cart, for the ghostly apparition had been directly in front of them and had materialized very clearly. Everything about it pointed to the Victorian era.

From then on, Bill, who had been an unbeliever, changed and never scoffed at anyone with a ghostly tale to tell from that day onwards.

The House of Despair & The Dom

There seems to be no rational explanation or justification for the haunting that occurred at a council house on the Lupset Estate, Wakefield, for, whoever occupied it did not stay very long and fled the area. Both couples involved in the haunting said that they would never go back to that house again. The first couple involved said that if they had known of the deaths there they would never have moved in, and wished that someone had informed them. Unknown to the second couple involved the phenomena had been witnessed by the previous tenants a few months earlier. After persistently questioning the neighbours, they found out that another family had been so frightened by the bizarre happenings, they had moved away to a completely different part of the estate. George said that if he had been made aware of the ghost he and his family would never have moved into the house.

The House of Despair

Upon viewing a council house on the Lupset Estate, Wakefield, John and Melanie Aisbett had different unspoken ideas from one another. John thought it would be perfect for them, but Melanie's first impression was that the house was scrutinizing her and she didn't like it, and that was only from outside. She dreaded going into the house and pretended to be interested in the garden and even then shied away from the big old tree standing at the front of the house. As a rule she loved to be near any kind of green foliage, but this tree gave her the creeps.

Shrugging aside her misgivings, she followed John to the front door where he unlocked it open for her to enter. There was no way she was going in first, and quickly made up the excuse of having something in her shoe, telling him to go ahead, she would be in shortly. After giving him a few moments, Melanie reluctantly stepped inside, but upon entering the house she immediately wished that she hadn't. She hated the place. 'What's wrong with me?' she thought, trying hard to dispel her fears. All she could feel was an intense urge to run away. 'This is ridiculous, come on now, this isn't like you,' she said to herself, and went upstairs to where she found John waiting.

Hand in hand they looked over the property, both upstairs and down. Then John dropped a bombshell that caused Melanie's heart to sink into her shoes; John thought the house was perfect. To Melanie it was blatantly obvious that something was wrong as the whole house emanated a disquieting air of depressive gloom that converged with the adverse atmosphere originating in the kitchen.

She didn't say anything to her husband of her fears and tried to put her anxiety down to the fact that the whole interior was in desperate need of redecoration, as the entire house was covered from top to bottom with drab wallpaper and dark brown paint. Desperately trying not to be put off with the dismal surroundings she put on a brave face for her husband, and against her first impressions and better judgement, told John that she thought that the house would be alright once it was redecorated, and agreed with him to take it on. It would prove to be one of the most unfortunate errors in their lives that they would ever make!

When they moved in the job of decorating fell on Melanie's shoulders, as John had a job that commanded flexible working hours. So, one morning after seeing her husband off to work, Melanie set about the arduous task of making the house more presentable and brighter by stripping the dingy wallpaper from the living room walls. Within minutes of her starting work a startling phenomenon occurred. As she was pulling at a length of paper she felt an icy cold sensation brush past her, and out of the corner of her eye caught a fleeting glimpse of something large and black that sped rapidly out of view behind her.

Immediately, she spun round fully expecting to see someone in the empty room, but to her amazement she was alone. Even so, her sixth sense told her that something was there, invisible it may be, she knew that there was a presence about that carried an underlying threat. Her hair bristled with fear. Terrified, she pushed her back up to the wall and edged her way to the open door, which she dashed through, slamming it shut behind her. Not daring to stop, she ran into the kitchen and banged that door too, before wedging a chair beneath the handle. "Oh, god, I need a cigarette!" she mumbled hysterically, "what am I going to do?"

Her hands shook as she fumbled in her bag for the packet,

and could hardly light it she was shaking so much. It was only after Melanie had taken a few deep breaths that she managed to calm herself, and as she made coffee began to wonder if she had over reacted. There could have been a reasonable explanation to what had happened, never the less, she could not bring herself to go back into the living room, and waited for John to come home before daring to enter it again.

Over the next few weeks the tension ensued. Her cat, which usually never left her side, would not enter the living room. He would scratch and bite if she ever tried to carry him in there. This was totally out of character as he was normally a gentle loving creature. Then, different types of phenomena began to occur, little things at first such as objects moving from one room to another, not being able to find things that they constantly used, anything that could cause inconvenience seemed to occur, and began to irritate them both causing them to argue.

Then things began to get worse. One evening, after they had finished their dinner and were washing up in the kitchen, a rack that was stacked full of pans suddenly lifted up and flew through the air towards them, scattering the pans all over the floor. Melanie screamed and fled, followed closely by John. There was no way the pair of them would go back in there until the following morning, and that was only out of necessity. Worse was to ensue.

One night as they lay sleeping in bed they were both woken by the sound of running water. Melanie leapt out of bed and rushed into the bathroom. All the faucets were wide open; water was gushing everywhere; the bath, the sink, even the toilet was flushing. "Oh, my god, what's happening?" she shrieked. Ignoring her outburst, John pushed past her and turned everything off, he then told her to be quiet and listen, as he had heard sounds coming from downstairs. "Somebody is in the house, stay behind me," he ordered. "If anybody is in the house, I'll sort them out."

Melanie watched anxiously as he stealthily crept downstairs, thankful of his six foot two height and massive frame. If anyone could deal with intruders, it would be John. Even though he had warned her to stay back, she was only two steps behind him when he threw open the kitchen door, where they were met by a scorching wave of suffocating heat. Gasping for breath, he reached out and switched on the light, then cursed at what he saw; the electric cooker was fully operative, the oven was working at maximum heat, the four rings were glowing red on the highest setting; the floor was flooded as water poured over the sink top. Angrily John splashed across the water logged floor and turned off the taps and cooker, then rushed about the house checking on all the doors and windows. Every one of them was secure.

Melanie crumpled in a heap of tears; it was all getting too much for her. From then onwards their health began to suffer; they couldn't get a good night's sleep, John cut off the end of his finger at work, Melanie suffered the loss of her unborn child. The house was slowly draining them of all their energy. They decided they had put up with as much as they could endure. They had only lived in the house for four months but the trauma and stress created there was to leave everlasting scars upon them both.

After persistently asking to be rehoused, the council finally gave in and they were relocated to a different area of Lupset. Just before they moved away everything was packed and ready for the removal men, when Melanie decided to take a last look around to make sure they had not forgotten anything. First she checked all the cupboards downstairs then went upstairs and checked the storage cupboard where, to her surprise she found a book lying before her, covered in dust. This was strange, for in the short while they had lived in that house she had never seen a book there before, and she had used that cupboard every day. Intrigued, she picked it up and blew the dust away from the cover, and found it was an old prayer book. As she held it a sense of well-being surged through her body bringing her close to tears, and as quickly as the emotion had come, it was gone.

Her thoughts were broken into by the sound of John's voice calling that the removal men had arrived and were ready to go. Sadly, she replaced the book and made her way down the stairs to where John was waiting. "Come on, love," he said, putting his huge arms around her shoulders, "let's get away from here." He led her to the waiting car to drive her to her new home and a new beginning.

Some weeks later Melanie happened to get drawn into a conversation with a lady who lived near the awesome property, who told her she was lucky to be out of that dreadful house. When asked why, she said, "Didn't you know? Before you moved in it was a death house." Melanie blanched. "The father, mother and son all died within twelve months of one another. Nobody would take it on." Melanie felt the colour drain from her face and her legs go weak. "Oh, my god, that's why we never got any peace in that house. I told my husband it was slowly killing me. We were lucky to get out when we did." The lady agreed with her, saying, "yes, you were lucky, very lucky indeed."

Second Haunting: The Dom

The first sign that something was amiss in the house came one late summer's evening. The weather was beginning to change and a slight chill came with the evening breeze, bringing with it the first inclination of autumn. At the time, 7.30pm to be exact, George and his wife, Jean, had just finished tidying away the dishes in the kitchen, when the temperature began to drop rapidly. Assuming that the coldness was blowing in through the open back door George walked over to close it before applying the lock and bolt. In the meantime, Jean had put the kettle on for a cup of tea. It was then that strange things began to happen.

While they waited for the water to boil they noticed that the glow from the light bulb was beginning to fade. At first it appeared to die out, when suddenly it brightened again, within a matter of seconds the bulb began to dim and glow at an alarming rate. The couple stood watching, their eyes glued to the bulb's strange performance expecting it to pop at any moment, when suddenly it faded to practically nothing, leaving only a tiny red glow emanating from the central filament. The bulb was left burning, but giving them no light at all. The only illumination that they had came in from the kitchen window. "Well," Jean said with a sigh, "I had better get another light bulb." No sooner had she spoken when she froze with fear staring towards the lounge doorway. George followed her gaze, and only just managed to put his protectively around her before the unidentifiable terror immobilised him also, and he gawked at what he saw.

Standing in the lounge doorway was the gigantic figure of a man, over seven feet tall, dressed entirely in black. On his head he wore a wide brimmed hat with a low flat top. On his feet was a pair of black boots that disappeared beneath a long heavy cloak that enveloped his massive shoulders and body. There was no discernable face, for it was masked by the concealing twilight shadows.

Paralysed and speechless they stared in abject horror when, with long, slow strides he began to move towards them. A weird preceding darkness was before him, and as he strode past, a brilliant blinding light emanated from his back that filled the room with such a stupendous dazzling brightness it caused their eyes to burn with pain. He then proceeded to disappear through the locked back door.

As soon as he had broken free from his transcendental confinement, George ran to the door. His hands trembled as he struggled with the lock and bolts, before finally managing to fling the door wide open, and he ran stumbling and shaking after the weird spectral giant, and was part way down the garden path when he stopped and thought, 'What the hell am I doing? I've just seen a ghost and I'm trying to catch it. I must be out of my mind.'

Turning, George staggered back into the house and slumped onto a chair at the kitchen table where his wife was now seated. "You saw it, didn't you? It walked straight through the bloody door!" Pointing, he said, "It came from there and went straight out there." Jean nodded in agreement and began to cry. George felt the same but managed to control his emotions for the sake of Jean. He rose and held out his arms to her, "Come her, love, let's try to make you better." Trembling, they clung to each other before suddenly noticing that the light was back to normal. "You go and sit in the front room," George said, "and I'll make us a nice cup of tea." "You must be joking," she replied, "from now on, there is no way that I'm going anywhere in this house unless someone is with me."

They moved away shortly afterwards, as they could not cope with the thought of the strange figure appearing again. George told me, "If anyone had come to me with a tale like that I would never have believed them, and I would have laughed. But seeing is believing and by God, I believe now!"

Is There a Connection?

Hanna Reed gave me a rather unusual story concerning her husband Adam, which transpired in the mid 1960's. This incident occurred before they were married. It was at the time when Ouija boards were at the height of fashion and popularity, where many people, with this unconventional method of entertainment were not aware of the consequences of the foolhardy game they were playing, and subsequently were to pay the price for their irresponsible behaviour, but by not only affecting themselves at the time, but of others whom they came to love later on in life.

There is an old saying 'Idle hands are the devil's advocate,' and although I do not believe there is such a being, I cannot help but wonder what on earth these people did make contact with.

On the day in question, Adam and his colleagues, who worked in York, had managed to get through their work load pretty early, and had nothing to do but sit around the office passing time with idle chatter.

Someone suddenly came up with the idea of making an Ouija board from cut out letters of the alphabet and a glass. Poor unsuspecting Adam was soon to be at the receiving end of a very unusual phenomenon. At first they all thought of the

Ouija board as a game, or, as one of them said, "A bit of fun." But later on, as their diversion from boredom progressed, some of the group became alarmed when the board began to spell out Adam's name, and was commanding him to go to a certain area of York at a specific time when a space ship would be landing. At first Adam said it was rubbish and that someone was playing a trick on him, and he refused to join in the group activities anymore. But even when he was out of the premises the board kept asking for him, and only after constant pressure from his colleagues did he finally relent, the reason being that his curiosity was aroused and it had become a serious matter, for the being controlling the Ouija board claimed to be an E.T.

It was too much for the group to comprehend, an ET claiming that a spaceship was about to land near York, in a village that none of them had ever heard of. No, there was no way that any of them could believe that. It sounded utter nonsense, but there was one way to make sure if the village did exist. A Map. None of them had an A-Z in the office, so Adam popped around to the nearby newsagent's shop and bought one. Sure enough, the village did exist, only a few short miles outside the city of York. With this information, the next time that they contacted ET Adam said he would go to the designated area, on the condition that he could photograph the spaceship. At this the being became extremely agitated and refused intimidatingly.

Adam declined to use the Ouija board again and would have nothing more to do with his friends, who were still contacting the self-professed ET, who was now telling them to go to the village at the appointed time. When the designated day arose, Adam began to wonder 'should I go, or not?' After a thorough analysis of the situation the thought of delving into the unknown did not appeal to him, and he sensibly decided against going to the appointed rendezvous.

The following day he was in for a big surprise, when he picked up the local newspaper and read in the headlines that a UFO had landed late at night on the outskirts of a little village just outside York, and had been witnessed by many people before taking off again. Thoroughly shaken, he stood staring at the headlines in disbelief, saying to himself, 'It was right, the board was right. I should have gone,' then quickly pulled himself together, 'yes, if I had gone, who is to say that I would have been standing here reading this newspaper,' and thanked his lucky stars that he had stayed at

home. But, he did just wonder who, or what, had they been contacting on the Ouija board? Had they really been in touch with some alien life form from another planet? He really believed that he had. But, had he?

Hannah, the girl Adam married a few years later was never told of this happening. Not until strange things began to occur in their children's bedroom did she begin to wonder if there had been some connection between the creature and the UFO, and contemplated what demonic form they had dragged up from hell with that depraved Ouija board.

In the late 1970's the couple moved into a self-contained flat above their business premises at Agbrigg, on Doncaster Road, Wakefield, with their three children, aged seven, eight, and nine. For the first few months everything was fine, but then the boys, who slept in the front bedroom, began to complain that their bedroom was cold.

Even with the heater on they could not maintain any vestige of warmth and asked for extra covers on their beds.

Hannah could not understand this as it was early summer and everywhere else in the flat was warm. All the same she had noticed that when the boys went out to play they wore the minimum of clothing, but when they came back in and went up to the bedroom they immediately put on thick woolly jumpers. At first she thought they were being silly as they were always up to some kind of mischief and she had ignored them.

It wasn't until the height of summer that she became concerned to see their pathetic little faces, white with cold each time they slept in that bedroom, and realised that it was no joke. Additional heaters were placed in the room and extra covers laid on each bed in an attempt to keep the children warm. The room was becoming increasingly colder and a disturbing sense of unnatural awareness saturated all who entered.

A few nights later they were awakened by horrific screams coming from the children's bedroom, and rushed in to find them shaking, huddled together on one bed sobbing with fright. "God, what's happening?" Hannah cried, clasping the children close, "Tell me."

"Mummy we saw a monster," sobbed the youngest boy pointing to the wardrobe.

"Come on, now," said his father, picking him up and

immediately felt how abnormally cold the child was.

"There was, dad," the eldest boy said, shivering, "it went into the wardrobe."

"That's silly," their father replied, "monsters do not exist, you must have been dreaming. It's with reading too many silly comics. Come on now, let's have you all back in bed, you are all frozen."

"But that's it, dad," said the eldest, "before we saw it we were all warm, but when it came we froze."

A shudder ran through Hannah. The sincerity in the boys' voices frightened her, and the tension in the room made her uneasy. She was reluctant to leave the children.

Adam could not comprehend what had happened to upset the children so badly and tried to ease the tension by saying, "you can have the light on for the rest of the night. Monsters don't like light, so he won't be back." With that promise the boys settled down.

The following night passed without any problems, but the next night was chaotic. Once again they were disturbed by the children's terrified screams, and rushed into their room to find them huddled together in a corner as far away from the wardrobe as they could possibly get, and had to take them into their room before they could acquire any sense out of what the children were trying to say. "I know that you're not going to believe us,"

The eldest boy sobbed, "but we had been asleep, and for some unknown reason we had all woke up together. I think it was the cold, we were freezing. Then this thing came out of the wall, it looked at first like a man, but when it came into the moonlight we could see that it was covered with scales, and then it went into the wardrobe. We saw from the back that it had a long thick tail with a point at the end. Dad, I don't want to go back in that room ever again." The other two boys echoed their reluctance to return also.

Adam considered the situation. "Well, we can't all sleep in this bed, so I'll tell you what we'll do. Seeing as Peter is the youngest, he can sleep here with mum. I'll sleep in this bed and keep you safe from the monster, how's that?" The boys were pleased with this suggestion and returned to their beds, confident that if the monster did return, their dad would sort it out.

The following day when the boys were at school Hannah asked her father if he would take a look around the boys room to see if he could find where the cold could possibly be coming from. She didn't dare look in the wardrobe. When he arrived she told him of what the boys had experienced. He put it down to an over active imagination and mass hysteria. One boy's fright had triggered the other two off, and scoffed at the idea of monsters, which did seem rather far-fetched in the daytime. Even so, he did it was too cold for the boys in that bedroom and told her to try swapping over for a few nights and see how they went on.

Hannah waited for Adam to come home and have his tea before approaching the subject of a change over. The idea didn't appeal to him; first, their room was too small for three beds and, second, he thought that the children were having nightmares, and to move would be meaningless, giving in to their childhood fantasies. From then on, as soon as the children arrived home from school or playing, the TV was switched off, and fantasy or horror comics were banned from the house. The children complained, but Adam told them it was for their own good as he believed that it was an accumulation of media rubbish that had frightened them.

That night, however, the monster reappeared, and was to do so at regular intervals over the weeks that followed.

It was now highly noticeable that the children's' health had begun to deteriorate. Each morning at breakfast they would sit hollow eyed, unable to eat, staring at food placed before them. In the end Hannah couldn't stand it any longer, and insisted they swap rooms. Reluctantly Adam gave in, and that weekend they exchanged rooms. The change in the children's behaviour was immediately noticeable, and they undertook a remarkable transformation within a few days and were perky and full of mischief once more.

Hannah, however, was not too happy, for her husband very quickly became depressed and could not rest. Apart from that, almost every night she was awakened by bright lights shining in her eyes, and upon switching on the light, no one was there. Throughout all of this the strain was beginning to tell on her husband, and he began to drink heavily. Finally, he couldn't cope with any more stress and, sadly, they separated.

The strange thing about it all is that after Hannah and Adam finally divorced she could never find any trace of him, which was strange, for he loved the children and had a good relationship throughout the divorce. They parted friends not enemies.

Could his disappearance be linked to the strange events

that occurred in his past with the E.T and UFO phenomenon? Had the monster really existed? Did that have some connection with the Ouija board? This is something we may never know.

The Portobella Phantom

A council house on the Portobella Estate, Wakefield, has been the setting for numerous hauntings over the past twenty years. In the early 1970's, one lady, Maria, a widow with two children, Sandra, aged 18 and Peter, aged 14, each witnessed the apparitions and phenomenon occurring there.

The hauntings seemed to be contained to just one room, a large bedroom where Maria had a large partition built so that the children could have their own private quarters. It was here; in the centre of the room where the partition was built that the apparition appeared.

In the past, Maria had often witnessed the manifestations, but had never said anything to her children about them as she knew they would have been afraid. But, one night, her daughter Sandra had a terrifying experience, coming face to face with the same ghastly spectre that her mother had seen. As she lay asleep in bed, something woke her and forced her to turn on her back and look up towards the ceiling. Upon doing so, to Sandra's amazement she saw a strange coloured glow appear that began to descend slowly lower and lower. Suddenly, in the midst of the glow a pair of shiny black shoes came into view, followed by white stockings to the knee black breeches, a white coloured shirt and cuffs. Hardly able to believe what she was seeing, Sandra sat up to get a better look. He had long hair, and a high black hat with a silver buckle central front. "It's a Puritan," she gasped. As he hovered in mid-air before her, he slowly opened his eyes and stared directly at her. They were blood red. "Oh, my god, please don't let it be there," she prayed, "make it go away. Let it be my imagination."

Quaking, she lifted the covers slightly so that she could peep out, but quickly dropped them back again, as he was still there staring at her. 'Oh, no, what am I going to do now?' she thought, 'I can't stay under the covers all night, I'll suffocate.'

There was only one thing that she could do, and that was to face it. Fighting the nauseating knot that had formed in her stomach and the hot jabbing pain that had developed in her head, she reluctantly pushed the covers away from her face and returned the man's horrendous glare. They held this defiant stance for at least another five minutes before the man began to elevate slowly back up through the ceiling, taking the strange glow with him. Immediately, upon his disappearance, a second figure began to emerge through the wall.

This one was a Cavalier from the King Charles period. Sandra could see every detail of his clothing and his features. He had long wavy hair and a sash around his waist. The only difference was that he illuminated a strange kind of darkness that concealed the colour of his white skin, clothing and hair, plus the fact that he had materialized only halfway through the wall, and stayed only a few minutes before he receded back from whence he came.

As soon as he had gone, however, the whole room reverberated in an explosive eruption of cannon fire that emanated from the centre of the room. Sandra could not believe what was happening and clung frantically to the bedcovers, hoping desperately that her mother would hasten to her. But no one came. Only she had heard the thunderous explosion that rang in her ears, she alone had witnessed the night's terrifying phenomena. The poor frightened girl sat up all night not daring to let herself drift to sleep for fear of the phantom's return.

When morning came, Sandra was relieved to hear her mother up and about and gratefully leapt out of bed and went downstairs. She was going to tell her mother about the previous night's experiences, but in the light of day she felt foolish, and decided not to say anything. It would have been better if she had, for shortly afterwards her brother, Peter, was to experience a different kind of phenomenon.

To the rear, on one of the shelves in Peter's bedroom, stood a modern cassette stereo radio. To the front of it he had placed a selection of beautiful glass ornaments that he had brought back from a recent holiday in Germany, and he was very protective of them. So much so, that he had implicitly expressed to his mother that on no account must she touch the ornaments or anything else situated on that shelf. He told her that he would clean and dust the shelf himself, which he dutifully did.

One night, as Peter lay in bed, he was unexpectedly awoken by the sudden shock of something heavy dropping onto his lower legs and feet. He immediately leapt up and switched on the light, fully expecting to see the dog on the bed. Instead, he got the shock of his life, when he saw the radio plus wire and plug laying there. "Oh, no," he groaned, "my ornaments."

Cringing, he dropped his gaze to the floor, expecting to see them all smashed to smithereens. But, they weren't, they were intact, still standing where he had originally placed them. Breathing a sigh of relief, he got out of bed and went over to the shelves and lifted one of them up. He could tell by the dust marks that they had not been moved. Then how come the radio was on his bed? There was no way that the radio could have been moved without first moving the ornaments. "This is weird, something's wrong here," he said to himself as he placed the radio in a corner on the floor, "I don't like this."

Feeling afraid he spent the rest of the night fitfully dozing with the light on, and told his mother the next day.

Because of Peter relating his experience, Sandra also told her mother what she had seen. Their mother then had to tell the children about the phenomenon that had been occurring there for years, and had not dared to tell them as they would have been afraid.

From then on the hauntings grew to such a crescendo that Maria's health began to suffer, and the children were becoming nervous wrecks. Finally, they could not cope with it any longer and had to move away.

Three years later I was told of another haunting that occurred at the same house by a different occupier.

Nancy

Nancy and her family were unaware of the previous hauntings when they moved into the house on the Portobella Estate. She never expected for a moment that her three year old daughter, Nicky, would become entangled in a mystery.

Two girls aged about nine and who were twins, became Nicky's ghostly friends. Nicky was to actually witness one of the dead children drowning.

Both her mum and Nan stated that this event changed her from a bright bubbly child to a sad, withdrawn little girl for a number of years.

The second haunting occurred in the early 1980's, when Nancy Burnham moved into the sinister house on Portobella Road with her husband and three young children.

The youngest son, Steve, had his own bedroom, and the two girls, Rebecca and Nicky shared the large bedroom that Nancy had divided with a curtain. One thing she had noticed about the room was that when she decorated it she found marks on the walls that suggested a partition had been built there at some time. This coincides with the first haunting, as Maria, the previous owner had a partition built in that room, but one of the following occupiers had taken it down.

The family settled in and within a few months the eldest children began to make new friends with the local families, while Nicky, the three year old who had always been mischievous and outgoing slowly became detached from everyone else, and began to spend a lot of time upstairs in her bedroom. At first her mother did not worry as the child had plenty of toys to play with and she knew where she was.

One morning, after Nicky had eaten her breakfast, she left the table and without a word to anyone disappeared back into her bedroom. Her mother thought it a little unusual but did not bother until she noticed that nearly an hour had passed and there was no sign of her daughter. Knowing exactly where the youngster would be she tiptoed up to her room and pushed the door slightly open so that she could peep inside. She saw Nicky seated on the floor with three cups and saucers from her doll's tea service set in front of her, and was engrossed in deep conversation with two unseen people. 'That's odd,' thought Nancy, as Nicky usually had her dolls out when she had a tea party and spoke to them. Now there was no doll in sight, so who was she talking to?

"Are you alright, love?" she asked her daughter, concerned. Nicky looked up, a huge smile spread across her face at the sight of her mother standing there.

"Yes, mummy, we are just having tea."

Nancy looked around the room and saw that her daughter was alone, and asked, "Who is we? Who are you playing with?"

"Oh, these are my new friends," she answered, standing up and held out her hand with a sweeping gesture, as if she was introducing someone to her mother. "This is Rosy and this is Christina, they have come to play with me. They used to live here before us, but in a much bigger house."

Bewildered, Nancy enquired, "What do you mean a much bigger house? Who are they? What do they look like?

Now it was Nicky's turn to look confused. She looked at her mother and then at her friends, then back at her mother. "I can't see them, Nicky. Can't you tell me what they look like?"

With an exasperated sigh Nicky gave her mother an odd look and began to describe the two girls. Both had long blonde wavy hair combed behind from the sides and held in place with a ribbon at the back of their heads. They wore long dresses with frills and their legs were black (black stockings) and on their feet they wore boots with marbles on the side.

"Oh," was all Nancy could say when the child had finished. "Well, I'll leave you to play," and she went downstairs shaking her head.

As the weeks and months filtered by, Nancy noticed that her daughter was spending more and more time upstairs with her invisible playmates. At first, she went along with her when Nicky insisted upon having her hair fastened back in the same style as the two girls, but became concerned when she constantly spoke of them to other people as if they were real.

The sad part was no one else could see them. Even her brother and sister began to ignore her, and left her alone. Being quite a bit older, they thought she was weird. In the summer time Nancy would go upstairs and ask Nicky if she would like to play in her blow-up paddling pool. Nicky would always reply, "Just a minute I'll ask Christina and Rosy if they would like to come." If they did, all well and good, but if not, then the child would spend all day indoors, thus upsetting her mother. No amount of coaxing or threats would bring her out of that room.

There was something that Nancy and her family found unusual, and that was that the girls did not age, and the only thing Nicky noticed different about them from time to time was that the girls wore either black or brown boots, with white over the tops of them, and were fastened with marbles. (It sounds as though she is describing spats). The girls were the same height, had the same features and dressed alike and were, perhaps, twins.

It was obvious that the girls did exist. Nicky could not have been making them up. From the age of three to her present age, a child so young could not describe people from the 18th century with such accurate detail as she did, and never vary her description of them.

From time to time Nancy managed to persuade her daughter to play downstairs or outside, and even on the rare occasion she would play with the children from the nearby houses, which was a great relief to her mother. Nancy hoped that some day Nicky would forget about her invisible playmates, but she never did. Then came the fatal day. Nancy had noticed that her daughter was not as boisterous as usual and had crept silently up to her room, avoiding contact with everyone. This was odd as the child always wanted to be centre of attention and this worried her mother. So, she gave her a few moments of time to be alone, then followed her. Her heart went out to her daughter when she saw her sitting alone with a look of anguish and misery etched upon her little face. "Nicky, what's wrong?" she asked. "Nothing," the child answered, pouting her bottom lip, fighting back the tears. "Come on, tell me all about it," said Nancy persuasively, "let's see if we can make it better," and cuddled her daughter on her knee. "Rosy has been naughty. Christina has told her she could not go out to play, it was not allowed, but she's gone out on her own and now she's drowned." Trying desperately to understand the workings of a child's mind, and thinking, how on earth can someone drown, who isn't there?

Nancy asked Nicky, "How do you know that. Who told you she was drowned? Did she fall into the river?"

Between sobs, Nicky answered, "no, Rosy fell into the water and drowned. Christina came and took me outside to the water, we tried to get her out. We couldn't reach her and she won't come out, and she's looking at us. Christina took me to help because she couldn't do it by herself. But I couldn't get her out of the water. Mummy," she sobbed, "she was laid in the water looking up at me. I was frightened because she would not move or listen to me, and she won't come out, so I had to leave her. Christina stayed with her and won't play anymore." The child was near hysteria.

Aghast by what she had just heard, Nancy held her daughter's heaving little body close to her, rocking and stroking her until she calmed down. She realised there was no way that Nicky could have concocted such a story as she was too young and too upset for her to have made up something as graphic and drastic as this.

Nancy now firmly believes what the child had experienced, and of the existence of her little friends. From that onwards Nicky was a changed little girl. She was terribly upset because the children never came back to play with her. Sadly, she became a lonely, melancholy child, and would often be heard saying to herself, "Rosy is under the water and Christina has to stay with her. I have nobody to play with anymore."

Intrigued at finding two completely different types of haunting at one property, I went along to Balne Lane library at Wakefield to see if I could find anything to connect them.

I had known of the famous battles that had taken place in the area as I live at Thornes, just across the river from Sandal and Portobella, where the battle of Wakefield was fought, between Cromwell's troops and King Charles 1st Cavaliers. After a long search I found that in 1825 a mansion that was named Portobella House, had been built on part of the battle ground. As the foundations were being prepared, human remains, swords, spurs, pottery etc, had been found at the site.

The records state that the house was built for Joseph Hume, a JP from Huddersfield. Strangely, through my search, I could not find out much about anyone living there. In 1925 it was sold to a Mr Sherwood, and in the early 1960's it was demolished and council houses built in its place.

I also found, that on a scale drawing on an old map of Portobella House, there was an old water filled quarry. This was situated not too far away from where the bizarre death of Nicky's ghostly friend had taken place.

I believe there is enough evidence here to substantiate both hauntings.

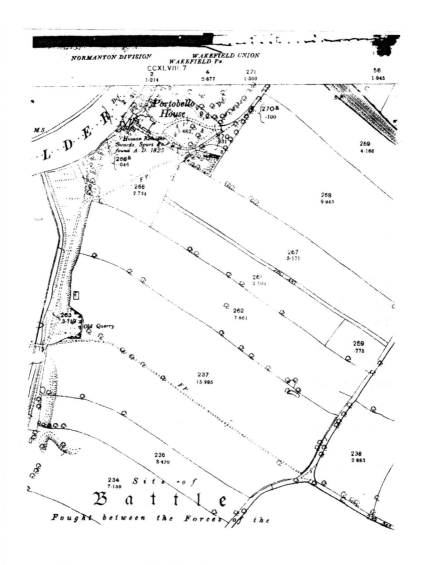

Map courtesy of Wakefield Library Archives, West Yorkshire

The Man with the Staring Eyes

Have you ever wished that you could see into the future? Some people possess the ability for a psychic vision, while others can see what is in store for them in dream form.

This lady's dream started in early childhood, when she used to live with her parents at Agbrigg, near Wakefield. It was to be a dream that would repeat itself over and over again, until 1986.

Mary Clarke had a very happy childhood, her parents lavished her with as much love and affection as any caring parents could upon their children. Every night they would tuck her into bed, where she was surrounded by all her favourite toys and the parent of her choice would read her a fairy story until she dropped off to sleep. Her bedroom door was always left slightly ajar, so that they would hear if she awoke and needed them. Life was perfect for the five year old. Until one night when her parents were alerted by their daughter's terrified screams.

They rushed upstairs to Mary's bedside, and as her mother held her, Mary told her that she'd had a nasty dream. Mary had been standing alone at the bottom of the staircase and when she had looked up there was a great big thin man with a moustache and glasses, staring down at her. She would not have been afraid, if it hadn't been for his big staring eyes. To take Mary's mind off the dream, her mother asked if she would like to hear a fairy story, and within a short time Mary was fast asleep once more.

As the days progressed, the same, frightening dream repeated itself, and, in time, it became a regular feature in her life, in as much so, that she became accustomed to the dream. Nevertheless, as Mary grew into a young woman, those large, staring eyes in her recurring dreams, never failed to unnerve her.

In 1974, Mary's father died, and in her sadness and grief, after the funeral, when everyone else was in other rooms of the house, Mary went into the kitchen to be alone. As she sat there fiddling with a half-cold cup of tea, Mary found herself compelled to look up towards the window, where she was astonished to see her father standing outside looking in at her. Her heart bounded with joy at seeing him once again, but before she could move or utter a word, he spoke to her, asking that she look after her mother for him.

Mary wanted to get up and take hold of her beloved father, but was helpless to do so, all she could do as the tears streamed down her face, was nod, then watch as he slowly vanished into a misty haze. True to her word, Mary looked after her mother throughout the following years, before marrying and having a family of her own.

In 1986, her mother began seeing another man, and after a period of time told Mary that she would like her opinion of him, as he had proposed marriage to her.

Mary agreed, and upon arrival at her mother's house on the

arranged day, while standing in the hallway taking off her coat, heard a man's voice say, "Hello, you must be Mary." On looking up to the top of the stairs to see who had spoken, her heart nearly stopped. Standing there was the man from her dreams; tall and thin, with a moustache and glasses. But the thing that struck her dumb was those large staring eyes. The man who had haunted her sleep since childhood was there, in her mother's home, and walking down the stairs towards her. Terrified, she nearly collapsed, and felt relieved to feel her mother take hold of her arm. "I don't think introductions are really necessary, do you, Mary? Not after all those dreams." After the meeting, Mary never dreamt of the man again.

The Man in Red at Walton

If you ever drive through the old part of Walton, near Wakefield, go along Walton Lane where you will see the Cenotaph standing at the crossroads. In the early hours of the morning it is a very quiet and lonely road, as there is no traffic or people about.

It was on this road that Stewart Guy was driving along at five o'clock in the morning, making his deliveries of newspapers to various newsagents in that area for the company he worked for, when a strange thing happened. As he approached the Cenotaph the temperature in his van began to drop at an alarming rate, leaving him bitterly cold and shivering. At the same time he saw a man standing in the early morning light, on the pavement alongside the Cenotaph. By now the temperature in the van felt as if it was well below freezing and his teeth began to chatter. Stewart could not understand how it had become so cold in such a short space of time, plus, it was a fairly warm morning.

As he drew alongside the man he perceived that he was dressed in a rather unusual style. He wore a black, three cornered tricorn hat over his long, wavy hair which cascaded down over his shoulders. His jacket was of a plain, red material decorated with gold and black braiding. The buttons were of shining gold. His trousers were also red and they were enclosed in thigh length black, leather boots.

The only unnerving aspect of the sighting came when Stewart had slowed down to take a good look at him. The man's piercing eyes had met his, as if seeking some kind of recognition. From that, Stewart got the impression that the man was waiting for someone. However, it was only after he had driven a few yards past him that Stewart suddenly realised that it was warm again in his van, and on looking in his driving mirror he saw that the man was watching him as he drove around the bend in the road.

'That looks like a Cavalier or a highwayman,' he thought to himself. 'No, it can't be," he argued back, even so his curiosity got the better of him. He swung his van around and drove back up the road, but as he approached the person standing there, he vanished before he could reach him. Feeling slightly unnerved, Stewart finished his rounds and quickly returned to his depot.

The Unknown Woman

Poltergeist possession can alternate between different people as shown in this unusual case. So, beware the person standing beside you, for the mind of a demon could be his, waiting to possess you!

Pandemonium was to break out one evening during a healing service at a spiritualist church in West Yorkshire, when an unknown woman approached Sid, the church minister, and his wife, Joyce, for healing. The peaceful conditions were to be disrupted and the congregation, healers and patients, were to look on in horror at what happened a few minutes after the woman had seated herself on the healer's chair.

Uncommunicative, she reticently sat staring into space, seemingly oblivious as Sid took her hands in his, while his wife, who was standing behind, placed her hands gently on her shoulders. Within minutes of body contact with the woman a terrifying phenomenon occurred. Sid's concentration was broken when he felt her fingers take a firm hold of his. Puzzled, he opened his eyes and lifted his head. "Good grief," he uttered, and his mouth dropped open with shock, when he saw that she was staring straight at him through rolled back, unseeing eyes.

As if encouraged by his mortified expression, a sly, lecherous grin spread across her contorting features, before her whole body erupted into a violent shaking mass of horror. At the same instant, a garish sound of coarse, obscene laughter emitted from her throat, causing everyone in the church to stop and stare in amazement at what was happening.

Repulsed by the sight, Sid tried desperately to pull his hands away, but her fingers had clamped around his in a deathly grip that squeezed and crushed, causing him to cry out in pain. Holding a mocking, menacing tone, the laughter became louder, then without any warning a forceful blow hit him in the stomach and he was hurled backwards for several yards across the church into a wall, landing in a heap on the floor, thoroughly winded. The woman was forgotten as people rushed over to Sid and helped him onto his feet, although he could not straighten up. The pain was so intense that it caused his legs to buckle beneath him and he had to sit down until the pain eased and he had got his breath back.

It didn't take him long to recover and stand up, when the woman came to his side and asked if she could speak to him. Surprised by her request after what had happened, he agreed, and was furthermore surprised to find that she was totally unaware of what had occurred. Subsequently, she told him that her name was Margaret and that she was experiencing psychic phenomenon in her home. She begged him to help her, then began explaining what was happening.

The mysterious happenings had begun two years previously, when one night as she was approaching her home she saw that the lights were going on and off in all the rooms.

Knowing that no one was in the house she ran up the garden path and hastily unlocked the front door. Throwing it wide open she stepped inside, and was immediately caught in a brilliant glare of light that suddenly filled the hall. Half blinded, she closed her eyes to adjust to the light, and then shielded them as she blinked painfully to look about her.

Nothing was out of place, except for the erratic behaviour of the lights. Puzzled, Margaret stood and watched as the bulbs slowly died down to a flicker of light that almost disappeared into nothingness, and then erupted into life again. At first she wondered if it was an electrical fault and proceeded to check the switches of every room and on the staircase. They responded to her control, but as she moved away from them the lights began to fluctuate irregularly. It was then that she started to feel uneasy. Fighting her fear, she hesitated for a moment before descending the stairs, not wanting to fall in the darkness, and waited for the lights to come back on again.

It was at that precise moment she felt a cold creepy sensation crawl across the nape of her neck. Simultaneously, a morbid sensation of doom began to evolve and circulate around her, and a strange, eerie stillness fell about the house. Terrified, forgetting about the darkness, she rushed down the stairs and came to an abrupt halt, when an ear-shattering blast of sound exploded from the radio in the kitchen. She nearly screamed but managed to keep quiet by pressing her shaking hands to her mouth, wondering if intruders had broken in and were playing games with her.

Desperately trying to keep calm, Margaret bravely pushed

the kitchen door open and looked inside, letting out a great sigh of relief when she found no one there. Turning her attention to the blaring radio, Margaret hurried over to where it was situated and reached over to turn it off. Before she could touch it though, there was a click and then it became silent. Stunned, she stood and looked at it, then nearly jumped out of her skin when it came back on again twice as loud, causing her to scream in both surprise and anger.

"That does it," she shouted, and pulled the plug from the socket, "I've had enough!" Grabbing the set she lifted it up above her head, and was about to smash it down onto the floor, when she heard music coming from the front room. "I don't believe this is happening to me," she cried. Putting the radio down she stormed into the front room, where she found the television, video, record player, radio and ever light, switched on and working. It was the final straw. She burst into tears and sobbed as she went around the house unplugging all of the equipment and turning off the lights that had unbelievably started to work normally, and went to bed.

The following day gave vent to turmoil and frustration for Margaret. As soon as she plugged the electrical appliances in they all went berserk. The hoover worked of its own accord, the iron would not cool down and steamed where it shouldn't, the automatic washer continually rinsed and the cooker ruined everything she tried to prepare.

In the end, she gave up and sent for an electrician, who spent hours trying to locate the problem a fault on the system. He examined each appliance but came up with nothing; everything was in perfect working order. After acquiring the services of various tradesmen throughout the following weeks and months, Margaret began to grow despondent, as no one could find a solution to the problem, so she turned to the spiritualist church to ask for help.

Sid sympathised with her and told her to come back the following week. In the meantime he would send out healing and peace to her home. When everyone had left the church that night, Mary and Bill offered to do the healing when the woman came back, which Sid gratefully accepted. He had suffered an angina attack a few months previously and realised that if another psychic attack occurred like the one that evening, it could possibly cause him irreparable harm.

The following week, the woman came back and allowed Mary and Bill to give the healing, but this time they were prepared. When the entity came through, the special service was put into motion, and it did not like it. The woman became sullen and unresponsive, the laughter stopped, and after many prayers had been said over her, they were relieved to see her begin to relax and the colour return to her cheeks. By the time the service was over, she was completely relaxed and said that she had not felt so well in ages. All the tension had left her face, the grey pallor was replaced by a rosy pink, and she was happy when she left the church.

The following day, however, Sid received a disturbing telephone call from Mary, telling about a weird experience that had occurred while they were driving home from church the previous night. As she was driving along the slip road after leaving the motorway, Mary had felt a waft of extremely cold air gush across the back of her hands. At the same time, the steering wheel was wrenched from her grasp causing the car to go out of control and hot another vehicle. Luckily, no one was injured, but when they arrived home, all the lights were on in the house, and all the electrical appliances were working. They had attracted the woman's entity!

The following Saturday, a hush fell in the church when the woman arrived and walked straight over to Mary and Bill. Instead of sitting down though, she told them that a great burden had been lifted from her; the entity had gone. Sid saw the look that spread over Mary's face and knew what she was thinking. As their eyes met, he had to turn away so that she wouldn't see him laughing, and swiftly retreated into the back room where he howled. Afterwards, Mary saw the funny side of the situation and had to laugh too.

The woman never came back to the church, and they never found out who she was or where she lived; it was as though she had never existed. It took a few sittings at Mary's home before they finally got rid of the entity completely, thus creating, dare I say, 'A Happy Medium.'

The Egyptian Amulet

Do you believe in the power of a curse? I do. I believe that the power does exist, as one came directly to me. An ancient one – from the tomb in the Valley of the Kings.

I have always admired the ancient Egyptian civilization, and have read many books on the subject of the Pharaoh Akhenaton and Tutankhamen. Akhenaton was classed as a heretic when he broke from the old traditions in religion, policy and art, and the priests hated him for it. Akhenaton introduced Monotheism to ancient Egypt, and only one God was recognised during his reign. The next King, Tutankhamen, came under tremendous pressure from the priests, so much so, that the old religion was re-introduced.

It was while I was reading about the boy King that I became interested in one article of jewellery that was found in his tomb. It was a gold amulet with a scarab beetle in its centre, that had been delicately carved from a precious stone. On either side of the beetle were two enamelled ibis in green and rustic brown. In all of his treasures, this one beautiful piece of craftsmanship, I adored. I would often get out my book and admire the amulet, and in the end my husband Eric asked if I would like one made for a Christmas present. Of course, I said yes!

The next day, Eric rang a jeweller friend of ours, who is a jeweller in London, and he came to our house the following week to see what I wanted. The date was October 13th. What a starting date! Everything began to go wrong. We had begun to argue for no apparent reason, our business began to go haywire and we were having trouble with our employees. Tom rang from time to time to let us know how the work was progressing on the amulet. He told us that there had been quite a few problems with it. He had to do all the work on it himself as his staff were hesitant in handling such a relic, even though it was only a copy.

Early in December he rang to let us know that he was having difficulty getting the amulet enamelled. It was a specialised job, and as he could not do it, he had to find another jeweller to take it on.

But no one would touch the work, saying it was evil and would bring bad luck to the person wearing it. As we talked, he enquired if everything was alright at home. I told him of the problems that had arisen. He said, "This may just be a coincidence, but we are the same at home and at work, everything has gone wrong. It's since I started on that blasted amulet!"

After we had finished our conversation, I sat down and began to think about what he had said, and about the amulet bringing bad luck. So, I called at the home of a lady I knew, Mrs Dyson, who had been (coincidently) in service at the Howard Carter household many years before. Martha told me that when the tomb of Tutankhamen was opened there was chaos in the Carter household. Back here in England, the dogs howled, his favourite one dropped dead, the horses were whinnying and kicking in their stalls, and strange sounds that could not be accounted for echoed around the house and property, sending fear into the hearts of everyone there. She warned me against the amulet.

Disregarding her words, when Tom rang informing me that he had found someone who would do the enamelling and be bringing it the following Monday, I agreed. We arranged to celebrate with friends on the coming Saturday. We would first go to a restaurant in Bradford and then on to a disco in Leeds. Saturday night came, and at 8.00pm we met up behind a parade of shops at the end of Petergate in Bradford, across the road from where we dining. Our friends had parked three cars behind ours, and then joined us to go over to the restaurant. By 10.30pm we had finished our meal, and after leaving we crossed back over the road to where both cars were parked.

As Peter and his fiancée were about to get into their vehicle Peter glanced towards us, and then stared in disbelief at the sight of me suddenly levitating upwards. At that precise moment I heard a strange whooshing sound and felt myself being lifted as I walked. I had at the time my arm linked through my husband's, but as I rose up my arm slipped through his. He stopped walking and looked on horrified as I was hovering between two to three feet in mid-air. What was occurring for only a few moments felt like forever before the macabre force released me in an aggressive manner by hurling me to the ground, where I fell in a tousled heap as my legs crumpled with the unexpected shock.

Peter said afterwards, that although he wanted to run

towards us, for some inexplicable reason his legs had become paralysed; he could neither move nor speak. Anna was petrified. All they could do was stand there helpless and shake as they watched Eric reach down to lift me. However, as he did so, from out of the darkness Peter witnessed a robed and turbaned man of eastern origin appear from nowhere, who took hold of my other arm and helped me to my feet.

The strangeness of the weird situation was the fact that I knew someone was there helping me, but when I looked I could not see anyone. Eric had also seen the robed man appear at my side as soon as I had been dropped, and had helped me to my feet. But as soon as I was upright, the mysterious man had disappeared. The very second the man vanished; Peter felt his body released from the restricting paralysis and rushed over to see if I was alright.

None of us could comprehend what had happened, the circumstances were so distressing that Anna burst into tears, Peter was suffering from shock, and Eric became overprotective and locked me in the car. What should have been a wonderful night out had turned into a terrifying ordeal.

The night's dancing had to be cancelled, due to the fact that left elbow was bleeding heavily, my left knee was also grazed and bleeding and I ached all over. Eric padded my elbow with both his handkerchiefs, and I had placed my lace handkerchief between my knee and laddered tights. Anna had become hysterical owing to the fear of something else happening, Peter was trembling so badly he could hardly keep a limb still, and Eric was the only one unaffected by the extraordinary happening. Nevertheless it didn't take much for each one of us to agree to abandon the night's entertainment plan, and after a tearful farewell went our separate ways home.

Leslie, our daughter, was surprised to see us driving in through the gate at such an early time. She had not expected us back until 3.00am, and feeling something was wrong, hurried out to the car as Eric put it in the garage. It was a relief to be back in the safety of my own home, where, as Leslie helped me out of my coat and evening dress, we told her what had happened. Luckily, Leslie is in the medical profession and she knew exactly what to do. She had seen that the bloodstained handkerchief lodged between my tights and knee was stuck with coagulated blood, and used warm water to ease it away from the wound. We were in for yet another surprise, for as the material came away there was no cut or graze showing where I had fallen. The skin was smooth and unbroken. We were totally baffled. She next took a look at my elbow that was still bleeding and advised me to go to hospital as there was a deep hole showing that may have needed a couple of stitches. I would not go. I don't like hospitals. So, she cleaned and padded the wound before bandaging it, and then packed me off to bed.

The following morning held another remarkable surprise. I was expecting the worst when I removed the bandage from my arm, but as I did so the padding fell away, and as I held my arm up to the mirror, I was astonished to see that the wound had healed itself. On the previous night there had been a hole on the very point of my elbow. The padding was stained with blood and so was the bandage. There was no logical explanation.

After breakfast we sat and had a discussion and decided that the amulet must go. Although it was Sunday morning we rang Tom and told him of our decision. He was pleased, and informed that a theatre company had been interested in the piece and by Sunday afternoon the amulet was sold and taken away. I was so sad and miserable that I cried for hours, partly from relief, but most of all from the disappointment of not having that beautiful piece of ancient Egyptian, handcrafted jewellery, that I had so long admired and yearned for. Nevertheless, some months later I was to receive a grim reminder of that fateful Saturday night.

I had felt something prickling my left elbow for a few days, and each time I looked there was nothing there but a red mark. Then a few days later I saw and felt two small lumps. Within a short time, two small pieces of bone broke through the skin and worked their way out. The chipped bones had dropped out of my arm exactly a year to the day of the supernatural phenomenon occurring.

The Stick that would not Leave Home

An old walking stick left in a derelict house seemed to have extraordinary powers. No matter how hard the new owner tried to dispose of it, it returned to its original place at the bottom of the stairs.

In 1985, Michael and his wife, Margaret, decided to buy a house in Sandal, near Wakefield. After months of patient searching they found what they were looking for. It was a semi-detached property overlooking a vast area of farm land, and was peaceful and quiet. The house needed a large amount of renovation, but as Michael was a builder it posed no problem, so they went ahead and purchased the property.

Before any work could begin, the house had to be cleared out as some of the previous owner's belongings had been left there. Everything was brought out and thrown into a skip that had been placed alongside of the property. Amongst the articles thrown away was an old walking stick, which had a hooked handle and a brass end fitted to it.

When the house was cleared the men then began the task of refurbishment. All of the internal doors were taken off so they would not get damaged, plus, it would provide easier access for the wheelbarrows to be pushed in and out and other large equipment needed there, as they had to strip all of the old plaster from the ceilings and walls.

After one of the men had filled the wheelbarrow with old plaster he began to push it through the open doorway, when something touched his face gently. On looking up he saw the old walking stick hanging directly in front of him. "Who put this here?" he asked his mates. They all shook their heads and one of them said that it had been put into the skip earlier that day. It should really have been at the bottom of all the rubbish. The man lifted it down, put it on the barrow of plaster and threw it into the skip outside. He then covered it with lots of plaster.

A couple of days later, as Michael was checking to see how the work was proceeding he was surprised to see the old stick leant up against the wall near the staircase without a mark on it. "What's this doing here?" he asked his men. "I threw that away two days ago," said one of them. "Well, I put it into the skip the first day we started here," another stated. They all stood looking at it, then Michael picked it up and flung it amongst the rubble. He turned around to his men, saying, "No more silly games. I don't want to see that stick in the house again." But a few days later it turned up again. It was leaning against the wall near the staircase, where Michael had first found it.

The men felt a little uneasy and began to talk amongst themselves, saying that the house must be haunted. None of them had taken it into the house after it had been thrown away, and if they were going to pull a joke on Michael, they would all have been in on it. "I'll get rid of it," one of the men said, and picked up the stick. When he got outside, the others watched as he pushed it as far down into the rubble as he could, then stood and watched as each barrow load of rubble was tipped over it.

The work progressed nicely as the days passed by, and the stick was almost forgotten. As Michael and the men were all working in one of the upstairs bedrooms, their attention was suddenly drawn to one wall in particular, and on looking they gasped in amazement. The old walking stick was back!

Michael was the first to move over to where it was leant against the wall. He reached out and lifted it, examining the stick to make sure it was the same one. It was. He was furious, "I can't believe it," he said, "we have thrown the bloody thing away, but it keeps coming back." "What are you going to do with it?" one of the men asked. "Nothing for now. I'll take it downstairs and leave it in the hall. He took it down and put it in the place where it seemed to favour turning up, by the side of the staircase, and returned to work.

They worked hard until lunch time, and then went downstairs to have their break. On reaching the bottom of the stairs Michael glanced over to where he had left the stick. It had gone. No one else had been in the house except him and his men. Puzzled, he looked around, but it was nowhere to be found.

The work carried on in the house and it was completed to their satisfaction. In between times, though, the old stick kept appearing for a short while, only to disappear again a few moments after it had been noticed by anyone. Everyone involved in the work there tried to ignore its presence.

Each time that it turned up, but found it hard to do so as it was slightly unnerving. The men also did not like to turn their backs on it once it was there, and although they tried to watch for its disappearance, not one of them saw it go.

The day finally came for the opportunity that Michael had been waiting for. The last load of rubble had been thrown into the skip and was being driven up the road. "This is it, lads," he shouted. With the old stick in his hand, he ran behind the skip wagon and threw it onto the back of the moving vehicle, and stood and watched as it was driven out of sight. The men cheered as he turned and walked back towards them smiling. Full of confidence and self-satisfaction he said, "That's it, lads, it's gone now. You all saw it go, it won't be back." Laughing and talking amongst themselves, they made their way back into the house to remove all the equipment that they no longer had any use for. Michael went in first and stopped dead in his tracks. Leaning against the wall at the bottom of the stairs, in its favourite resting place, was the old walking stick!

Hardly able to believe what he was seeing, he turned, mumbling garbled words to the men behind him and pointed to the mysterious object. The men beat a hasty retreat down the drive, quickly followed by Michael.

Before long, the house was decorated and the furnishings were set in place, and they finally moved in. throughout the months that followed, the stick would put in an appearance. Each time it was noticed, a member of the family would either put it in the outside garage, or in a cupboard. At other times it would be placed in the dustbin, but it would still return to its favourite resting place at the bottom of the stairs, and it would be perfectly clean. What the family did find amusing was that Michael, who suffered from gout, discovered the stick would turn up either two days prior to an attack coming on, or in the middle of a severe bout. It came with such precision timing that now he no longer fears the stick's appearance, but dreads it.

Michael has his own stick that he has used for about four years, but when he needs it he can never find it, but the old one appears. In early August, 1988, Michael opened the boot of his car and got the shock of his life, lying on top of everything there was the old walking stick. It was the first time it had turned up somewhere different from its usual haunt. He dreaded the thought of what might be to come in the next couple of days.

He did manage to find out from his neighbours that the old walking stick had belonged to a Mrs Beaumont, an elderly lady in her early nineties, who had died there eighteen months previous to them buying the property. The neighbours had often seen her walking very slowly about her garden, leaning on her stick for support. Perhaps it is she who is leaving the stick for Michael to use, as people from the spirit world can sometimes give us advanced warning of things to come. Both Michael and Mrs Beaumont have something they can relate to, and that is, the stick!

When Time Stood Still
& Who is John Ritchie?

Time stood still for Sylvia when she was whisked away by an unseen force. It was the first time she had experienced any type of phenomena. On her second encounter, in her time of need, did her guardian angel offer her comfort as she lay entombed in the mangled wreckage of her car?

She believes she did, and after hearing her story, I am inclined to believe her.

At the age of ten, Sylvia Dunford experienced a strange phenomenon in her home town of Middleton, Leeds. It occurred in the late afternoon in the summer of 1956, while she was on her way to visit a friend who lived just a short distance away. As she walked along the street acknowledging friends and neighbours and dodging traffic, she felt a strong irresistible magnetic force of power pulling at her, compelling her to look up into the sky. She saw a huge silver disc shaped object hovering directly above her. At first she could hardly believe what she was seeing, and turned to look at the people in the street, fully expecting them to be witnessing the same as her. But, no one else seemed to be aware of it. Baffled, she returned her gaze to the incredible sight; it was still there, how could they not be seeing it?

It was then that the strange phenomenon took place. It was as if she had stepped into a great void of timelessness, for even though the public and traffic were passing her by, there was no sound. Everything had dropped still and silent, she actually felt as if she wasn't there. It was the weirdest thing she had ever experienced.

The presence of the space craft appeared to have taken away all normality of life, in fact she felt quite numb, and it was as if time itself had ceased to exist. This inconceivable feeling stayed with her for at least half an hour before she was released, when the craft unexpectedly zoomed away at high speed, and within seconds was out of sight.

As it left, Sylvia felt as if a great weight had been lifted from her mind, and a surge of relief flooded through her as she became aware of the sounds of voices and the steady drone of traffic as it sped along the main road, echoing through her ears. Thrilled at what she had witnessed and bristling with excitement, she looked around at the faces passing her by, and was amazed to find that no one else appeared to have seen the space craft.

Being so young, she dared not mention the sighting or what she had experienced during the sighting, so she kept her secret to herself.

However, a few days later, a friend of her father's, Bill, had dropped by, and in casual conversation he laughed and joked as he told her father that he believed he had seen a space ship over their street. Sylvia could not contain her secret any longer and told the two men what she had seen, describing all the details and times it had occurred. Both sightings and descriptions corresponded in every detail. Sylvia said there was no way that craft could have been engineered on this earth; it was too advanced in its size and speed for anyone here to build.

Who is John Ritchie?

The second extraordinary incident occurred in the winter of 1981, following a road accident. At the time, Sylvia was trapped in the crumpled wreckage of a van she had been driving. A snow clearing wagon had skidded on snow and ice onto her side of the road, down a hill at Green Lane, Methley, and hit her vehicle head on.

As she lay entombed by the mangled metal which was wrapped about her legs and lower body, an electrifying tingle of phenomenal energy coursed through her body, and in the flicker of an eye, she found herself floating above the carnage looking down at the two vehicles which were locked together as if in mortal combat. As she marvelled at her new found capability, Sylvia underwent yet another startling phenomenon that was one of unequivocal tranquillity, where every feeling of fear, worry and pain, ceased to exist. She was at peace with herself and the world, until something occurred to cause her great concern. Without warning, an unforeseen force began to pull her further and further away into an unfamiliar terrain.

At first she didn't understand it, but as the sensation grew stronger, realization seeped through her new found euphoria. She was dying, and began screaming, "No, no, I don't want to go, please don't take me. I want to stay."

The next moment she was back in her car looking out through the shattered windscreen watching tiny flakes of snow fluttering all around her, and shivered as an ice cold wind blew about her shoulders, emanating from the broken windows that had partially fallen from her vehicle. She also became aware that the engine was still running. Instinctively, in spite of the pain, Sylvia reached out and turned the key, even so, the engine still functioned. 'Oh, god, what am I going to do?' she thought, and reached for the door handle. The doors were wedged tight due to the impact of the crash.

Poor Sylvia was crying out in agony and desperation with no one to assist her, when two young men appeared.

One of the men, Bill, disconnected the battery leads, whilst the other forced the car doors open and knelt beside her, holding her hand trying to comfort her. He said his name was John Ritchie, and managed to convince her she was going to be alright and that help was on its way. This young man gave Sylvia a great deal of encouragement and confidence, and, as he held her hand, she swears that she could feel the strength emanating from him and flowing into her body. Bill also held her hand and reassured her that everything would be fine until the emergency services arrived.

Upon hearing the sirens Sylvia wept, for she knew her ordeal would soon be over, and as the teams came to her, John stepped to one side. After what seemed like an eternity, Sylvia was finally pulled free and rushed to the hospital. A few days later, she was pleasantly surprised when Bill called with a big bunch of flowers to see how she was progressing. As they talked, Sylvia asked about John who had forced open the car doors, saying that she would like to thank him personally for helping her, and did Bill know where John lived?

Bill was completely baffled, and told her they were alone throughout the ordeal. "No," she stressed, "there was another person." Sylvia proceeded to describe him; tall and slim, with dark brown hair and eyes. He wore a flat cap and dark jacket. He had stood towards the front of the van watching until she was released. There was something strange though, that she remembered quite clearly; she had been looking at John all the time the crew were freeing her, and he was watching her. But as they placed her on a stretcher he had disappeared.

Bill shook his head. "I was the only person there with you until the police arrived. Perhaps you mistook one of the officers for him." Sylvia was adamant, "No, he was there!" In due course they ended up having a disagreement as both were convinced that they were right.

After leaving hospital and convalescing, Sylvia set about the arduous task of searching for her mystery helper, and knocked on practically every door in Methley, but could not find him. She even went as far as asking her solicitor to employ a private detective, and sent him out to the surrounding area. She also placed adds in the local newspaper, but he was never traced. It was as if the man had never existed. Regardless of this, Sylvia is still absolutely positive that John Ritchie does exist, and, who are we to question her?

It does make you wonder, however, what guise do guardian angels come in? To Sylvia, whichever way you look at it, John was an angel in every way.

The Drowned Girl at Ackworth

A haunting can be caused by many things, but we usually find that grief or tragedy is the main reason. It is the shock of passing quickly from our earthly life that causes us to remain earthbound and carry on as we used to do in our past life.

Can we ever understand what it must feel like to die suddenly, to be cruelly murdered, or die in a terrible accident? To sink to the bottom of the sea, or some murky river or quarry, to slowly die alone?

I do not think we can.

Eve and Alan Soar moved into their brand new home with much excitement and enthusiasm. It was in a brand new block of flats that had been built at Ackworth, near Pontefract. Although they had decorated and furnished it before moving in, they had never noticed anything unusual about the place.

It was not until they had been living there for a few days that Eve began to notice something strange. She could not explain it at first, but it was as if someone else was in the room with her.

One evening as the couple were sat in the lounge watching television, they both felt the presence of a third person in the room, accompanied by an overwhelming feeling of sheer panic and terror. The feeling stayed for only a few brief seconds, before fading away leaving a strong aura of tension in the room.

The pair of them glanced quickly about the room, and then jumped up. Eve voice quivered as she asked her husband, "Did you feel that?"

"I certainly did. What on earth do you think it was? I've never felt anything like that before," he mumbled. "I don't know," she replied, shaking. This was to be just the beginning.

The strange phenomenon began to occur nearly every evening, and as time went by, they started to get used to it, although they could not understand what was going on. Then, something different happened.

The couple had finished their evening meal and were sitting in the lounge talking, when suddenly the usual feeling of terror began to arise, but as it did so, something touched the back of Eve's head. Startled, she jumped up and turned, expecting to see someone standing behind her, but no one was there. "My god, something touched me!" she exclaimed. "Did you see anything?"

"No," replied Alan. "But I felt it, there was definitely something here." Filled with apprehension, they both settled down, but this time it was an uneasy atmosphere.

The next few days and nights passed by peacefully. Then, one day, while Eve was alone in the flat, a different sensation came. Waves of anguish, sorrow and misery washed over her. It felt as if some invisible being was there desperately trying to communicate with her. Inwardly, she felt herself responding. The being was so close now that she wanted to reach out and hold whoever it was close to her, to give love and consolation. Without warning, the presence became visible.

A lovely young girl aged about eighteen or nineteen, was standing in the room with her. She had long, blonde hair that fell straight down her back. She was wearing a calf-length dress and her feet were bare. Although the girl was looking straight at her, Eve could not remember what the girl's features were like or the colour her clothes. Her only certainty was that the feeling of panic and fear was receding from the girl, giving way to a wonderful feeling of peace. After a while, the girl slowly made her way across the lounge and disappeared through the door.

When Alan came home, Eve told him what had happened.

"At least we know what it is now," he said with relief. The feeling of panic and fear had completely disappeared, and whenever they felt the young woman's presence, it was a sensation of calm and peace from that day on.

The only occasion when Alan caught sight of the girl was one evening as he was seated reading in the lounge. He felt a sudden impulse to look up, and as he did so, he saw the girl go floating through the closed door. He got up and opened it, but to his disappointment she was gone.

On other occasions she would stand behind Eve and touch the back of her head, and then go away. Sometimes, small objects would be found to have moved from their original settings, and would turn up elsewhere in the flat at a later date.

The couple decided to investigate, to try and find out who

the girl was and why she was haunting them. Upon making enquiries, they discovered that the flats had been built upon an old disused quarry, which was always full of water and at times flooded. It was at one of these times that a teenage girl had been out walking barefoot alongside the water's edge, when suddenly she slipped and fell into the water. No one had been about to hear her cries for help, and within no time at all, the poor hapless girl soon sank to the bottom of the cold murky water and drowned, thus giving rise to the feeling of sheer panic and terror that the couple were experiencing in their home.

Since the young woman had started to show herself to Eve the haunting began to taper off. Perhaps she has found peace at last through Eve being so receptive, thus making it possible for her to materialise. Eve had given her the love and compassion that the poor girl had so desperately needed, releasing her from the ghastly event that had taken her life. At least she seems to have found peace.

Three Boys and an Ouija Board

Here is proof that children should never be left without a parent or some person in charge to look after them and to keep them out of mischief.

When Tracie Lindsay and his friend, both aged eight, along with his fourteen year old brother, made up their own Ouija board consisting of a glass surrounded by the alphabet, they got the fright of their lives.

It was 9.00pm and time was dragging that evening for Tracie and his pal Jim. They had become bored and needed something different, something adventurous to do, so they asked Tracie's older brother if they could play with the Ouija board. Tracie and Jim had never played the Ouija board before and being inquisitive youngsters, they wanted to know what it was all about. His brother agreed, and in no time at all he had set up the glass and alphabet ready to start.

Trembling with excitement, the boys placed their forefingers onto the upturned glass and waited as their brother asked it questions.

At first nothing happened, and after a time the boys grew bored and were about to give up, when, suddenly, the glass sprang into life spelling a man's name. However, as soon as it had given the name the glass shattered into tiny pieces, half scaring them to death. Thoroughly alarmed, the boys froze, not daring to move as they sat staring in horror at where the glass had been.

That one episode was enough to stop them from using the Ouija board again. Even so, as the days slipped by, the boys could not get the name of the man out of their minds, and wondered if it was he who had shattered the glass. In the end they spoke to someone older who went with them to Pontefract library, where they searched through old newspapers that were stored on micro-film, in the hope of finding his name.

After days of continually scanning through roll after roll of film, they finally came across the gruesome details of what had happened to him, and blanched at what they read; the man's macabre demise had occurred in Tracie's own home, and to make matters worse, in the kitchen where they had been playing with the Ouija board. The kitchen was built over garages with a twenty foot drop to the ground.

The poor sad soul had strung a rope above the kitchen window before launching himself into empty space. There was no chance of survival.

The boys were saddened and ashamed, yet it taught them a lesson. It was wrong of them to have used the Ouija board, and they vowed never to touch one again. One possible reason for this phenomenon occurring could be that the man returned in such a scary manner in an effort to protect them from the dark side, and to ensure that they would never use the Ouija board again. We will never know what drove him to commit suicide.

I do believe that creatures from different realms are constantly awaiting admittance into our time and presence. Therefore, gullible people, who do not know how to use psychic protection when using these means of communication, allow these creatures to be drawn amongst us when accepting messages from the Ouija. Nonetheless, as soon as contact is made with what is presumed to be the dead person, they are actually making contact with the demonic side who are pretending to be the deceased.

Therefore, by accepting the messages, these creatures come forth and wreak havoc in people's lives, causing bad luck, depression, madness and suicide.

YOU HAVE BEEN WARNED

Poltergeist
The Soul Stealer

The word 'poltergeist' is enough to send shudders down the spine of most people. It is a dark and dangerous force that should not be tackled alone. If anyone has a problem with this, then outside help must be sought immediately.

A poltergeist phenomenon is usually brought about by playing with an Ouija board. It is usually the lower side of life waiting to come through and can pose as a loved one, a friend or relative that someone is grieving for, or desperately trying to contact.

For some silly people it is just a game, but the consequences can be severe, as once it is accepted by any member of the group it can cause havoc in their lives and homes. So beware and leave well alone!

It seems to be an impossible undertaking when trying to educate the public of the danger concerning Ouija boards. The horrific consequences were brought home to bear, when two of the women, who took part, out of boredom, in the shameful ritual of commanding the dead to communicate with them through an Ouija board, received more than they bargained for. One of the women, Sandra, who knew that she was psychic, should have known better, for she had already undergone many weird and mystifying experiences throughout her life.

Every other evening a group of four young couples would meet at each other's homes, where, after they had eaten, the husbands would go out for a drink leaving the wives to pursue their own activities. The activity in question being the Ouija board, which was taken to each person's home to provide the evening's entertainment.

The men knew what the women were doing, and one night decided to go back to the house earlier than usual, where they stood to one side watching and listening to what was being asked. Suddenly the board began to spell out 'death,' 'death,' 'death,' and each time it was asked for whom, the pointer would spin crazily about the board.

Brenda, who owned the board said, "That's it! We have had enough. If you are going to carry on giving this message we are going to stop now." Immediately, the pointer went to where it should be and became still. To be honest, they were relieved and had another drink before cajoling their husbands to join in the fun and games.

When the men asked the board questions it made its own comments that were nothing to do with the questions put forward. It told of personal and private affairs that were only discussed in the privacy of each individual's home. The men could hardly believe what was happening, and asked the women if this occurred all the time. No, it had never done this before. It was only since the men had joined in that the board had ever responded in this way. Two of the husbands got up, declining to go any further, when they started playing again. It was Brenda's husband who stopped the repugnant farce from progressing any further, when the board stated that his wife's dead grandmother was communicating with them, and gave out too many intimate details of their lives.

He had heard enough, as he realised that something deeper than normal was working amongst them, and told his wife that the board must be disposed of, saying he did not want her messing about with it ever again. The evening was ruined and each couple made their way home wondering and worrying which one of them was going to die.

For the following weeks not one of them could sleep or work properly due to the Ouija board's messages. Brenda had thrown the board into the bin after that night, expecting all her worries to be over. How wrong she was to be.

A few days later, when they returned home from work, they were appalled to find that ink had been splattered all over the bedroom walls and covers of their freshly decorated bedroom and new bedding. "Why the devil is it, that whoever has done this has picked the cleanest room in the house," her husband complained, before checking on all the doors and windows for a sign of forced entry. Everything was secure. The television, video and all the essential electrical equipment was in place. Nothing had been stolen or tampered with. There had not been any visible intruders.

The incident was pushed to one side, but one evening supernatural happenings began while they were watching television. The companion set on the fireplace began to rattle and sway from side to side. After watching it for a while, Brenda picked it up wondering what could be causing it.

Traffic was not the answer as they did not live directly on a main road. The fireplace was even and so was the set.

A few days later it did it again, only this time it lifted up in the air and they could see beneath it. Horrified, they realised what was happening and could only wait until it lowered, before settling down on the tiles once more. Irritable and shaken, Brenda escaped to the bathroom not wanting to witness any more phenomena, only to find herself fraught with another problem; all the bottles on the bathroom shelf were sliding and vibrating. Terrified, she ran back to her husband, only to be confronted with the companion set floating in mid-air and him sat boggle eyed staring at it.

The incidents kept on occurring over the next few weeks and continued to get worse, with objects and ornaments falling from the walls, furniture and cupboards. Nevertheless, the worst type of phenomenon was yet to come.

It happened late at night when all was still. As Brenda lay sleeping beside her husband, she was rudely awakened to find something the size of a man clinging to her back. Sheer horror and panic raced through her when she tried to get up and found she couldn't. The malevolent venomous creature was holding her down and she could not move. The whole room was filled with an intimidating sense of evil.

Brenda realised as she lay paralysed and helpless that the being was attempting to fuse into her body, to become part of her. Fear was her worst enemy. Inwardly screaming and hysterical her mind suddenly became blank with shock, her body numb. In what had felt like hours, but was only seconds, Brenda became aware of herself praying. Inwardly she said the Lord's Prayer over and over again. Then without warning, she heard herself saying out loud, "Deliver us from evil, for thine is the kingdom, the power and the glory." As she spoke these words, the creature released its grotesque grip from her body. It was still beside her but not touching her. Tears coursed down her face as the strain became overwhelmingly unbearable. Why didn't her husband wake up?

Somehow she knew that the power of good was also alongside her, and with renewed strength and confidence she continued to recite the Lord's Prayer until the creature dissolved into a vaporous mist and was gone. Only then could she awaken her husband before finally breaking down into screaming hysterics.

While all of the pandemonium was progressing in Brenda's house, Sandra was also having problems. They had commenced shortly after her mother's death. Due to her husband working abroad and the children away at boarding school, Sandra was alone in the house when the first onslaught occurred.

She had retired early to bed that night, taking with her a cup of coffee and some magazines. Upon entering the bedroom Sandra had opened the bedroom curtains, thus allowing brilliant shafts of moonlight to flow into the room, lighting up everything in there and creating a warm, comfortable atmosphere. Sandra had dropped straight off to sleep. Cocooned in the comfort and warmth of her bed, Sandra began to dream, and in that dream someone was repeatedly calling, "Sandra, Sandra, Sandra" In fact, the voice became so pitched and intense that it finally jolted her awake.

Startled, she raised herself up onto her elbow and looked about the bedroom, thankful that earlier on she'd had the presence of mind to open the curtains. Even so, she could still hear the voice, and realised, to her dismay, that whoever was calling her name was there in the bedroom with her and invisible. By now, Sandra was fully alert and felt her heart somersault when it called to her once more, this time in a pleading, whining tone, "Sandra! Sandra! I want you to come with me. You will like it here, please come with me."

At first she had not recognised the voice as it sounded muffled and unclear. However, when it did become more comprehensible she realised that it was her mother speaking to her. Again, it called, even more urgent this time, begging for her to follow, and began echoing all about her, making it impossible to pin point where the sound was coming from. Suddenly, without warning she became paralysed, and in the same few seconds, felt herself being drawn from her bed as if by a giant vacuum. Mentally she fought against it, but it was no use. In the split second that the force had dragged her from the bed she was aware of herself being propelled towards the bedroom door, and could hear her mother's voice constantly calling for Sandra to come to her.

Sandra felt herself being dragged rapidly down a long dark tunnel, her body twisting and turning as if she were as light as a feather. In sheer desperation and panic she screamed, "I don't want to go with you, I'm not ready, I don't want to go." The next thing she knew, she was back in bed, thoroughly soaked in perspiration, exhausted and out of breath, and unable to move, as the paralysis was still holding her body rigid. For a while time seemed to be standing still, then swiftly as the force had engulfed her, it suddenly departed, leaving her weak and completely drained of all energy.

When Sandra told me of this incident, she said, "I was not dreaming, and although it is a terrible thing to say, I will swear on my children's lives that I was not dreaming. I know the difference between a dream and reality. I know that if I had said, 'Yes, I will come with you, mother,' then I would not be here today, I know that I would have died. But, I will say this; some part of me went that night. I really do believe this. I cannot say exactly what it is, but I feel as if part of my soul has gone."

A few weeks after the voice event, Sandra was to undergo another traumatic ordeal. Once again, she was alone in the house, as her husband was away, working in Hong Kong. She had gone up to bed early, and had read her book before setting down for the night. As she lay in the darkness, she began to feel lonely and her thoughts drifted off to her husband, who she loved, and wished that he was there by her side. Unable to sleep, she began to make notes in her mind of what had to be done that week, and what she would wear the following day.

Suddenly, her thoughts were disrupted when she became aware of another presence in the bedroom. At first, Sandra thought that Tim had come home unexpectedly when she saw the figure of a man standing in her room by the dressing table. To her surprise, an unusually highly exaggerated sense of security overwhelmed her as she lay watching the shadowy frame. Whatever appeared to be her husband took off his jacket, got undressed and hung his clothes up in the same manner as Tim, before walking over to the bed, and sitting down on top of the covers, which she found unusual as Tim never used to do that. He would pull back the covers and then sit down.

She felt the bed sink under his weight and spoke to him, but he did not answer and stayed in the same position. It was then Sandra realised that something was very wrong and she pulled the duvet closer to her as the comforting sense of security rapidly ebbed away.

What happened next was to cause her to be held in a stark terror that she would never, ever, forget. At first, the man turned slowly before sliding under the duvet and wriggling over her, straddling her vulnerable form. In that instant she knew that it was not her husband, it was not even human, just a solid mass of volume that seemed to change its shape at will. Spasms of fear shuddered through her body when the being leant over her and began pulling the duvet tightly across her throat threatening to choke her. Unable to scream or cry out made matters worse and her panic deepened as coloured lights began to flash in the darkness, when at any moment the increasing pressure on her larynx threatened to asphyxiate her. She closed her eyes, not wanting to look at the creature which was drawing her life from her, and at the same moment an inner voice was also telling her that she must not look upon its face.

In those first horrifying moments Sandra found that she could not think straight, her brain had become disorientated, and she could feel herself beginning to slip away. Miraculously, for some unknown reason, as Sandra's body became relaxed, the creature released its aggressive hold upon her. It stayed, hovering in its dominating position and she felt it slowly leaning backwards. Sandra opened her eyes and stared awestruck as the creature simply just drifted away and evaporated before her. The moment she was released, she switched on the light and jumped out of bed. Whatever had been on the bed had now gone.

Sandra's legs wobbled like jelly as she dragged herself out of the bedroom to the safety of the lounge, away from the terrible creature's presence, switching on every light as she passed. Her entire body shook from head to foot with shock, pain and the fear of the creature's return. Nothing on this earth would entice her to go back into that bedroom. Sandra dare not tell anyone of her ghastly experience, for she was afraid that people would think her mad.

But, a few days later, a frantic phone call from Brenda crying, "Please come, I dare not leave the house, and I don't want to stay here on my own," sent her racing to her friend's home, that was only a couple of doors away from her. When she arrived, Brenda was in a terrible state of hysteria, and it took Sandra quite a while to calm her down. However, when she did, she was shocked to hear of the creature clinging to Brenda's back, and immediately connected it with the creature on her bed.

They then discussed everything in minute detail of what happened in both homes, and agreed that the same creature had visited them, and that something had been taken from them with its visit. Also, they were in no doubt that the overwhelming sense of panic seemed to appease the creature, when it realised that it had complete domination over both women.

It took some time for Sandra and Brenda to recover from their ordeal. Anyhow, when they felt well enough they spoke to some older residents in the area and discovered that the land their homes were built on was part of an overflowing graveyard. With this knowledge in mind, the pair of them realised what they had brought upon themselves by playing with the Ouija board. They have now learnt their lesson and will never touch one again. Sandra and Brenda have only three words to say to the gullible public who are about to dabble with the Ouija board, 'LEAVE IT ALONE.'

It is in my opinion that Sandra and Brenda were visited by a demonic force known as THE INCUBI, which was brought forward from the outer realms through the Ouija board.

The Incubi was feeding from their souls, their emotional energies, for when they reached the climax of their fear, and felt as if they were about to die, it stopped. The Incubi knew that it had drained every last bit of that particular energy from them. This is what it fed upon; FEAR.

It never visited them again. One thing I do believe is that the creature is still there, patiently awaiting its next unsuspecting victim.

Don't let that victim be you.

Chance Encounters with UFO's

What links UFO sightings to the appearance of the Dom? There is a certain apparition that on many occasions is either seen before or after a UFO sighting. I refer to it as a Dom, as it always reminds me of the figure on a particular bottle of port. The Dom makes a sensational appearance in either a spectacular blinding white light or plunges the whole area of where he appears into the pits of darkness, and only he is visible.

As I have always concentrated on the spiritual aspect of my investigations, I am now finding that the two phenomenons are somehow interlinked.

In the early 1970's, when our youngest daughter became critically ill, we began to have severe poltergeist activity in our home, this was when the Dom began to appear at regular intervals in just about every room in the house. I asked for help at several local churches, but was refused, so I turned to the spiritualist church, but, whenever they approached my home they said something was blocking them and they dare not enter. The phenomenon carried on for a further ten months, which by then was affecting my own and my family's health. We had given up all hope of receiving any help from anyone, when, one day, there was a knock at my front door. I was surprised to see a man and a woman in identical clothing standing there. Both were tall and thin, they wore dark grey, almost black suits and trilby style hats. On their hands they wore extremely thin black leather gloves that appeared moulded to their hands.

Although I looked at their faces, I could not seem to focus on their features. I remember thinking at the time,' how on earth did they get through the gate when I had two guard dogs outside?' In the short space of time they were with me, the only words spoken were by the man, who said, "You are deeply troubled and we have come to help you." As soon as he had spoken I burst into tears and brought them inside, where he immediately took both of my hands in his and held them for a few moments. He then released my hands, and standing directly in front of me took hold of my head just above my ears and held me in a firm, yet gentle grip, where I felt we had merged into one being.

Within seconds I began to feel the pressure in my head build up, and then suddenly a great surge of power flooded through me followed by a huge sense of relief, as whatever it was shot out of the top right-hand side of my head.

All the stress and tension that had been building up inside of me over the past two years was gone. The next thing I knew was that I was alone. I could not remember them leaving, or hearing the gate open or close, and neither dog had barked. When I went outside I found the dogs cowering in their kennels and they would not come out.

From that day on all the heavy phenomena ceased from our home and all the outside buildings too. Until that day I had an extremely high psychic ability, but after their visitation my powers became very weak and have taken many years to rebuild. Sadly, they have not been on the same level as they were before.

UFO over Doncaster Road

About a year after my experience in the mid-1970's, Leslie and I were driving along Doncaster Road –this was before the construction of the M18. The time was between 8.30pm-9pm on a late summer evening, when I saw an object in the sky and said to Leslie, "That looks like an aeroplane in trouble and is going to crash," as it was spinning around and flashing different coloured lights. Leslie looked and said, "No, it's a helicopter." I replied, "But it can't be, it's too high up and too big to be a helicopter." I swung the car off the main road and positioned it facing upwards on a sloping embankment. I switched on the main beam and wound the window down, then stood outside, reaching in the car to flash the main beam in the craft's direction.

To our surprise the craft began to descend in our direction following the full beam of my car headlights, before it stopped. Although it was still very high, we could see that underneath it had a huge pulsating white light in the centre, while smaller red, blue and green lights were slowly revolving around it that were set in like a silver metal.

Above this was more metal that was spinning at a rapid rate, then another part shaped like a dome that was stationary with windows that shone with strange blue white lights. Once again it began to descend, and we could see it was enormous, the pulsating white light alone would have covered a full acre of land. No sound or smell came from it, nor did it cast any reflecting light or shadow on the ground below. I felt no fear as I watched it come closer, but Leslie began screaming and was so hysterical, that I reluctantly had to drive away.

Once we were back on the road, however, and she had regained her composure, I asked if she could see any sign of the UFO, but she couldn't. We were in for another surprise though, as drivers coming from the opposite direction began to flash their headlights at us and pointed upwards. Sure enough as we suspected when we looked up, it was there directly above us. I followed the contours of the road, the craft staying above us, until we reached the village of Ackworth, where it rose almost in slow motion and skirted the village, as if keeping us in its sights.

As we neared the end of the village and the farm land emerged once more, I decided to stop and take another look at it, whereby some other drivers blew their horns at me, while others shouted to get in the car, for the simple reason being, they had watched as it hovered overhead, and as I stopped the craft had stopped also. Much to my dismay however, the craft suddenly zoomed high into the sky and disappeared.

When we arrived home I contacted RAF Finningly, where I was informed unofficially that there had been numerous sightings of the craft in the Yorkshire area. The following day we found out that all the electrical systems of my Jaguar car were completely burnt out, and the mechanic could not understand how we had managed to get home without incident.

Almost a week later I was informed by the same gentleman at RAF Finningly that the craft had been seen travelling along the Norfolk Broads, and they had tracked it until it had disappeared over the sea!

Leeds M1 Motorway

In 1990 one late summer night at about 11pm I was driving home with my friend Margaret, after visiting some people we knew out at Collingham Bridge, and had just driven onto the M1 motorway at Leeds. As we approached Stourton we saw directly to our left a large silver cigar shaped object travelling alongside of us that had suddenly appeared out of nowhere. It had a long narrow strip of fluorescent lilac light that ran across the centre full length of the craft, which met at its centre and bounced off itself before returning to either end.

It continued in this manner and stayed alongside of us until we reached the junction of the M62 motorway, before veering upwards and disappearing into a heavy dark grey cloud that evaporated. The sky was clear with no clouds, except the one that appeared from out of nowhere. We were baffled!

UFO over Sandal Castle

In October 1992 between 6.30pm and 7.00pm I was in the study talking to my daughter on the telephone, when my attention was drawn to Sandal Castle, which is just across the river from my home, when I observed a number of large, red glowing discs in the sky. I told Leslie what I was seeing and put the phone down so that I could contact one of our neighbours from down the lane to witness the strange phenomenon.

He arrived within minutes and we stood and watched outside at the strange light formation as it hovered above the castle before zig zagging upward in an erratic motion, then zoomed away at lightning speed disappearing from sight.

My husband, who had been out walking the dogs down the lane, had stopped to watch them too, while the two German shepherd dogs cowered behind him in fright. As soon as they were gone, the dogs raced home and wouldn't leave the house.

Sandal Castle Hill

In June 1993, I was upstairs on the veranda polishing the patio doors and glanced over towards Sandal Castle, when I witnessed something very unusual. Numerous balls of silver white light were shooting down from the sky and disappearing into the hillside of the castle.

Fascinated, I watched for a while, and then dashed downstairs to grab my camera, and was lucky enough to get some good clear shots of them. The next set of lights that appeared descended with jerky movements at lightning speed that suddenly merged into one huge ball of light. Then, as it approached the hill it slowed to a crawling pace, orbited the castle and the hill before dissolving into the dome of the hill.

For some unknown reason none of the photographs that I had taken could be developed. I received a blank roll of film. I have never had any trouble with that camera before, and it is still in good working order, so what happened to those photographs?

UFO over Denby Dale Road, Thornes, Wakefield

Friday, July 19th 1994, I was in my garden when I saw two silver discs UFO approaching from the north. These were immediately followed by six Chinook helicopters flying at lower level, all were travelling in the direction of Emily Moor, Holmfirth.

Within minutes of the sighting all of the electrical appliances stopped working in my utility room. Our cars and heavy goods vehicles and all of the electrical items in the commercial garage were drained of energy.

The following Saturday, white plasma-type balls of light, the size of large tennis balls, were seen by family, friends and our drivers, floating above the rear of the house and garages before dissolving into the buildings.

Eastmoor Estate, Wakefield

On the 6th of February 1995 a young woman was driving home from work with her father when they saw a brilliant blue white light shoot across the sky over Eastmoor.

As it passed over the estate all the street lights in its path shut down for a few brief minutes, and all the security lights of the residents' houses switched themselves on.

This was witnessed by many people on the estate.

M1 Motorway

A night in February 1995 was clear and cloudless as Leslie and I travelled along the M1 from Birmingham towards Sheffield. At the time Leslie was driving and I had just looked at the clock, it was 9.25pm.

As we approached junction 25 I saw a pale blue light coming up behind us, and as it was a steep gradient and the light was further back up the hill, I thought it was a police vehicle approaching.

Yet within seconds the whole area of motorway was illuminated in a blue white sparkling light as a massive UFO passed overhead.

Then it paused and slowed down for a few seconds, allowing the sparkling white light to fade from around itself. We could hardly believe what we were seeing. Cars were all over the road and horns blaring as people slowed to stare at the gigantic glowing aquamarine saucer.

All of a sudden the UFO began to glow again with the curious white light, and then shot forward at a tremendous speed, stopping abruptly. It repeated this action twice before shooting away, leaving a sparkling white vapour trail behind as it headed in the direction of Stocksbridge.

The speed of the UFO was phenomenal. Nothing built on this earth could move or manoeuvre as swiftly as this craft did.

It was not of this world!

The Tannery Lane Ghost

In the late 1980's weird happenings frightened the work force of a motor spares department, which was situated on a modern industrial complex in Leeds, when heavy commercial and car parts began to move of their own accord.

The spares department is positioned at the rear of the car showrooms, and covers a large area of ground, where you will many rows of shelving over ten feet high, that contain every conceivable part for company's vehicles and its customers. With the parts being stored at such a height, and being extremely heavy, the only way possible to remove them is by forklift truck, while the more manageable items are carried down by the use of a step ladder. It was in this department that Ian Smart experienced the disturbing phenomenon.

It began late one afternoon while Ian was assembling an order that was to be delivered early the following morning. While he was checking the invoice he felt a strange tingling sensation run up and down his spine, and the hairs at the back of his neck began to prickle and stand up. He spun around fully expecting to see one of his workmates standing behind him, but no one was there.

Turning his attention back to the order he tried to concentrate on what he was doing, but the eerie feeling persisted setting his teeth on edge and his hands began to shake. He could sense a presence, and a morbid fear arose in him as he felt himself being scrutinised by an inhuman hostile being. With a feeling of foreboding he waited for a hand to fall upon his shoulder, but it never came. Then, as soon as the phenomenon had begun, the tension it had created began to ebb and quickly flowed away.

Breathing a sigh of relief Ian leant over his work bench forcing himself to relax, and nearly collapsed with fright when he heard the sound of footsteps padding about on the concrete floor behind him, followed by the heavy resounding thump of heavy objects being dropped to the ground.

"Who's there? What do you want?" he called. There was no answer.

Steeling himself, Ian involuntarily forced himself to walk between the rows of shelving towards the direction of where the sounds had come from. Upon reaching it, he stood in shocked amazement staring at the shambles before him.

Various vehicle parts were strewn in disarray all over the floor. Some of the items contained glass and mirrors that had dropped from a considerable height. But on examination, Ian found that nothing had been cracked or broken, nor was any of the packaging crumpled or damaged. Normally, when something drops from a height onto a concrete floor there would usually be some sign of damage, but none of the boxes had burst open. He was stunned and could not make head or tail of it. He replaced as many parts as he could, leaving the heavier objects where they lay before returning to his desk.

He had no sooner begun to work when he was disturbed

once more by the sound of footsteps and objects falling to the ground. "That's it," he shouted. "There's got to be someone else in here," and ran towards the commotion. But as soon as he got there the sounds stopped, and again parts had been strewn about in all directions. "This is ridiculous," he said, and shouted for whoever was causing the disturbance to stop. In his anger he had not felt the atmosphere beginning to change, but as he did so his skin began to crawl and his heart palpitated, with the dreadful realisation that the invisible intruder was there alongside him. This time he did not stop to put the parts back on the shelves as survival instincts took over. He was off like a bullet out of a gun.

Much later, when I an had calmed down, he returned with a colleague

To visit the phenomenon, but much to his relief the activities had ceased. A few passed before the strange occurrences began again. This time it was with two people working together in the storerooms. It was the same as before with the footsteps and parts being thrown about. Ian was pleased that it had happened to someone else, thus confirming his own experience.

On occasion some of the store men had been mystified when they heard the sounds of heavy chains clatter to the ground, but upon investigation the chains have still been in their original places. In other areas of the department where there were no chains, the sound of chain being dragged along the floor and clanking noises had been heard. It was understandable that the men went in pairs to check out any unusual sounds.

There could be an easy explanation, for I found that the complex was built on an old tannery site. An old lady I spoke to in the cemetery across the road from the complex told me that there had been fatal accidents in the past at the tannery, and the site had also been, many years ago, an overflow graveyard for plague victims.

If there are plague victims or accident victims haunting the complex, then I believe that the works' employees are lucky to be just hearing the noisy phantoms, rather than seeing them.

The Dark Arches, Leeds

I always find the dark arches of Leeds mysterious and intriguing, and wonder how many different crimes have been committed there over the centuries in its dank, infested, gloomy cavities. How many shifty characters involved in shady dealings have met an untimely end, after being cast into the fast flowing river that races through the arches, and were swept away never to be found?

It was here that Adrian Gibbs received the shock of his life one sweltering afternoon in the early 1990's, whilst working at his business premises, situated in the dark arches of Leeds. At the time, Adrian was sat talking with members of his staff in the office and happened to look up and glance through his two-way mirror. He saw a short stocky man, with thick black hair and a long black beard speckled with grey, wearing a calf-length black overcoat, enter his shop.

As he watched, Adrian thought it rather odd that he was clothed in such a manner, due to the fact that it was such a hot day, yet the fellow was dressed for winter. Adrian kept his eye on him, and observed that the man hesitated for a couple of minutes, before proceeding to walk all the way up the centre aisle of the showroom, and was only a few feet away from the office, and was within eye contact to Adrian, when he became transparent and then disappeared.

Adrian couldn't believe what he had seen and ran into the showroom with his assistant, who had also seen the strange man and searched the whole area for him. But he was gone. There was no possible way for him to have left the premises other than the way he had come in. Even throughout the search, Adrian knew that it was futile as the man had dissolved in front of him, and returned to his office slightly unnerved to resume working.

On my second visit, to pick up my order, I actually saw the man walk through the screened wall at the rear of the showroom, and was surprised when informed that there were more arches behind the business premises. Adrian also pointed out where that, where the man had gone, was close to a door hidden behind the screen which Adrian always kept locked. However, upon his unlocking the door and entering the neglected unkempt arches, was akin to stepping out into an ear long past.

The air was cold and rancid, and a malevolent aura clung like a shroud to our very senses, causing us to shudder as we forced our eyes to focus, in the unaccustomed surrounding darkness. It was then that I saw him, standing very still, as if waiting for someone. This time, however, instead of holding the briefcase in his hand by his side, he suddenly lifted it and was clutching it to his chest in a defensive stance, as if someone was about to take it from him, or he was protecting himself with it.

Something next occurred that was rather weird. The man froze in his position. I stepped forward, regardless of his unseen assailant to get a better look at him, but, due to his face being covered by his bushy whiskers and the darkness, I couldn't make out much, only that he was Jewish and in his mid-fifties. He held the same stance for a few seconds longer then faded away into the darkness. Another lady who works for a business in the dark arches has seen him, but does not wish to be names as she is afraid of ridicule.

A Nightmare Vision Comes True

Due to a disturbing dream and the distressing circumstances that followed, Melissa had a very clear recollection of the times and dates of all the nerve-wracking events that were to occur three months later in May 1967; events that would change her whole way of life and cause her, a young mother of three children, to have a heart attack.

It was also to cost her marriage, and to cause her continually suffering and great sadness through to this day. Her most hear-rending statement was; "The day I lost my mother was like the end of the world."

It certainly was, as it nearly killed her!

The extraordinary dreams began while Melissa was living with her husband and children in a flat in Wimbledon, over the surgery where she worked as a dental secretary. Her work was very demanding and at times, at the end of the day, she would collapse into bed completely exhausted and drop into a deep sleep.

It was on one of these occasions after a mentally and physically exacting day, that she had gone to bed early and roped into a deep sleep. Almost immediately her head touched the pillow she began to dream.

In her dream she experienced the exhilarating sensation of

weightlessness, as her astral body travelled through time and space to an unknown location, where she found herself floating near to the rafters of a strange old building. On looking down, she realised that she was in a small church filled to full capacity with people and flowers. The congregation overflowed into the vestibule and outside as far as she could see into the churchyard. 'What's wrong, why am I here?' she thought, as she hovered overhead.

Suddenly, without any warning her thoughts were interrupted as she began to drift slowly down towards the altar, where she eventually found herself positioned beside two coffins standing side by side that were covered with clusters of beautiful red roses.

As she stood there, alone and invisible amongst all the gloom and depression that surrounded her, an agonising sadness reached into her heart causing her to cry out. Somehow she knew that she was connected with the awful melodrama that was taking place before her. Then, from out of a dark corner of the church a priest appeared and began to conduct the funeral service.

Although Melissa was standing close to the priest she could not hear a word that he was saying, nor hear the rustle of paper as the congregation leafed through the pages of their hymn books and began to sing inaudibly to the silent chords of the organ music. The whole service was being conducted in a macabre eerie silence. Just as Melissa began to wonder if the strange ceremony would ever end, the pries turned and lay down his note book. Almost as he did so, a group of pallbearers stepped forward from a dark shadowy recess, lifted the two coffins to their shoulders and carried them outside to their place of burial.

Once again, Melissa found herself floating, and observed a huge crowd of people standing in the cemetery and surrounding area. She had never seen so many people at one funeral; even more mystifying was the heavy presence of police officers who were mingling amongst the crowd of mourners. She knew that there were bizarre circumstances about this funeral, but could not understand why she was witnessing them.

Even when she hovered above the open grave, she could not recognise any of the chief mourners as they stood and wept when the two coffins were lowered into the ground. However, as the second coffin was interred, a great surge of anguish and suffering overwhelmed her with so much pain, that she awoke thrashing about in her bed in absolute agony.

In the few months that followed, Melissa found it very unnerving to be assailed by different aspects of the dream, but none with which she could indentify. She had been in touch with her parents and everything was alright with them, so she was not too concerned, until May 18th.

It had been a beautiful day and the sun was still shining, even though it was 5.30 when Melissa checked her watch. The surgery was empty and she was ready to pack up and go outside for a breath of fresh air when suddenly it became very cold in her office, the gauge on the wall showed below forty degrees and dropping. Feeling a little frightened and apprehensive she sat perfectly still not daring to move, when she became aware of a presence standing close by her side. At the same instant she watched mortified as a spiral column of smoke came whirling softly towards her, gradually becoming larger until it enveloped her quaking body. Gritting her teeth she sat and waited, fully expecting the worse when something strange happened.

All of the fear she had been experiencing was wiped away, and a wonderful sense of peace wrapped itself about her, comforting her like a mother with a young child. She immediately recognised the feeling and remembered her mother's words, "When I die, I will let you know, for if there is a way back, I will come to you." She knew that it was her mother coming to tell her that she had passed on. Upon recognition, the presence and the smoke faded away.

The following day Melissa decided that as her parents did not have a telephone, she would travel up to Leeds and make sure that everything was alright. She had finished work early, had packed an overnight bag and was ready to leave, when the doorbell rang.

Hoping it was not a late patient; she opened the door and was surprised to see two police officers standing there. One of the officers was a stranger to her, but the other she recognised as the Sergeant from the local police station. "Hello, Melissa. May we come in for a moment? He asked. A pang of fear twisted in her stomach as, by the look on his face, she knew that something was badly wrong. "Yes, of course, come in," she said, and stood back allowing them to enter.

"I think you had better sit down," the Sergeant said. "I'm afraid I have some bad news for you. It's about your mother." Melissa felt herself wobble and his hand supporting her until she was seated. With great compassion in his voice he spoke the words that were to haunt her for the rest of her life. "Melissa, your mother is dead." She sat there nodding, numbly agreeing with him. "I know, I know," she repeated over and over again. His voice seemed to come from another dimension when he said, "Your father is, also. You must prepare yourself for a shock, Melissa, but we think they have died under suspicious circumstances." "Oh, dear god, no!" she shrieked. "No, it can't be true." Melissa dissolved into floods of tears and there was no consoling her. Melissa was devastated; she had loved her mother and step-father.

The grief and suffering that she went through in the next few days, weeks and months was indescribable. Nothing could console her, she was crushed with sorrow.

The following day she journeyed north to Leeds to identify her parents' bodies, and suffered untold agonies as she stood in the cold, unwelcoming atmosphere of the mortuary. Everything seemed so unreal. 'This can't be happening to me,' she thought as a sob broke in her throat. 'It just can't.' Suddenly she felt the room begin to spin, and became aware that someone was supporting her, as she was led away from the pitiful remains of her parents.

The inquest was the next distressing event. Numbly she sat listening to all the bizarre circumstances leading to her parent's deaths. After that came the ultimate ordeal; the funeral, which was take place on May 26th 1967. As the cortege drove through the cemetery, Melissa commented on the multitude of people gathered there. But it was not until she was seated inside the church that something clicked in her brain; recognition of her dream.

The small church was filled to its capacity and overflowing with people, the masses of flowers and two coffins standing side by side covered with beautiful red roses. She had been in the church before, she had seen it in her dreams, and as the priest came forward to begin the service, for the first time she recognised him standing there in his robes.

Everything had fallen into place. She had seen it all three months earlier, but had not realised that it would be her mum and dad, the two people she had known and loved all her life, and all the bizarre circumstances of their deaths. She thought that it was a nightmare. Her dream was a nightmare; a nightmare vision come true.

Dreaming of Daffodils

In 1965, Sylvia Poore of Baildon, awoke one morning feeling very distressed over the disturbing circumstances of a dream she had just had.

She had dreamt that a family friend and neighbour, Mr Weir, had died that night. The dream had been so real and vivid, that while she was telling her daughter, Susan, about it over breakfast, she broke down into tears as she relived the sorrowful event when describing the vast amount of daffodils that had been placed upon and around the coffin.

"Come on now, mother," her daughter said, her voice filled with compassion. "It was only a dream and he was alright a few days ago when you saw him, wasn't he?" Sylvia nodded her head. "Well, then, you don't have anything to worry about do you?" In spite of her nagging worry, Sylvia decided against ringing the family. However, that evening when the family were seated at the table eating, her husband said, "You will never believe who died last night, Mr Weir."

Sylvia turned to Susan, whose jaw dropped at the sudden, unexpected news.

"Now then, what did I say to you this morning? Go on; tell him about my dream last night." Susan's voice quivered when she told her father, "Mum dreamt that Mr Weir died last night.

She told me this morning at breakfast."

At the funeral, daffodils were arrayed in abundance about the coffin and church, just as she had seen in her dream.

The Angel of
the Holy Trinity Church,
Knaresborough

This strange but beautiful phenomenon occurred when Brian Beucard and his brother James were playing football on fields at Knaresborough in 1938. The wondrous event was also witnessed by their group of friends who, to this day, remember every last detail of the angelic being that appeared above them that night, before disappearing into the church steeple of the Holy Trinity Church.

For Brian Beucard, his brother James and group of friends, football was the ultimate goal in life. They could hardly wait each day for three thirty to arrive, knowing that they would then be free from the constraints of school and free for a game of football.

As soon as the school bell rang the lads would grab their belongings, race home, get changed and gobble a sandwich down, before charging off to meet at the local cricket field where they would wait for each boy to arrive, and then climb over the padlocked gate and commence their game, each boy pretending to be the player that he idolised.

Completely engrossed in the game, time slipped by unnoticed to the youngsters as the darkness of the night began to descend upon them. They were pushing and jostling one another about, when Brian shouted for them to stop and look at the strange object approaching the sky over York Place. The boys could hardly believe what they were seeing.

From about four hundred yards away, in view for all to see was a sparkling yellow ball of light, surrounded by a brilliant golden glow that lit up the whole area as it floated slowly towards them. The game of football was forgotten as the glowing object drew closer, but as it did so, it began to change its shape, becoming vertical like an egg.

Upon reaching them it stopped as if it wanted them to draw into their minds every aspect of its being. For as it did so, the boys perceived what was inside the nucleus, that had now become transparent. One boy saw hands and feet, another saw a head, outstretched hands and feet, while the rest saw a perfect angel of celestial beauty with white feathered wings. Awe struck, the boys stood immobilised by the mystifying vision above them, and as if the angel knew that the memory of her visitation was buried deep in their minds forever, she once more began to move and gently floated over their heads.

The hypnotic spell was broken. "I'm going to tell my dad!" Brian yelled, and ran for home with his brother James in hot pursuit. "Dad, there's an angel on the cricket field," Brian shouted, as he barged in through the back door. "Honest, there is."

"There is, dad," James commented breathlessly. "It's coming up Iles Lane now!"

Their father looked up at them from his newspaper shaking

his head and said, "Don't talk so daft."

Brian interrupted, "There is, dad. It's outside now, come on, have a look."

"If you two think I'm going outside looking for angels you've got another thing coming. Now take yourselves off and play, or have a clout and go to bed."

Disappointed, the two boys raced out of the house and rejoined their friends, and then saw that the angel had by now passed over three streets and had cut over the top of Iles Lane. The illumination of the angel's aura filled the night sky, dimming the light from the old gas lamps with the brilliance emanating from her. The angel then disappeared over the top of a row of houses known at that time as Garry Houses, which stood in the churchyard behind some trees. The boys had to run down another street to be able to see her again. This time she had stopped moving and was hovering above the Holy Trinity Church, before entering one of the top belfry windows.

The whole area was surrounded with the brilliant glowing light that followed her as she descended to each lower level, and then she was gone. The lads stood for ages outside the church, waiting in the hope that she would reappear, and talked about what they had seen. They also made an agreement not to say anything to anyone about the sighting, for they knew from Brian's dad's reaction that no one would believe them, so decided to keep the secret to themselves.

It would be nice if more people would come forward like Brian, for in this day and age, an angel sighting is an accepted phenomenon.

Premonitions
The Loud Speaker
The Snake

The question is often asked, 'Can we be forewarned of impending danger?' I say, 'Yes, we can.' It is a form of extrasensory perception, an inborn instinct of self-preservation that is built into every human being, to give us an insight of what is about to happen, to alert us in our moment of need.

The man in this story had two premonitions of impending danger. He did not heed the first and was hurt, but the second intuition saved his life. The first incident occurred when Mark, at the age of sixteen, attended an Open Day with his mother and grandmother at his younger brother's school. At first everything was fine, but upon entering the huge school hall, where the speeches and presentations were to be made, Mark became extremely agitated and nervous, and felt an uncontrollable urge to run from the building. Fighting his rising panic he stood still for a few moments to regain his composure, and swept his gaze around the hall, over the rows of chairs placed for the visitors and stopped when he saw the loud speakers directly above where his family had seated themselves.

Mark knew instinctively that this was where the danger lay, and when his mother asked him to join them he shrank back in horror saying that something bad would happen if he sat there, and could not be persuaded otherwise. In the end she gave up, but his grandmother, who was a very persuasive lady, managed to coax him into sitting with her a few chairs away from the others. With great misgivings, he sat with his shoulders hunched and waited for the inevitable to happen, and it did.

Within seconds of his being seated, the heavy loud speaker above him dropped from its fitting in the wall and landed on his head, injuring him and knocking him unconscious. There was a great commotion as he was rushed to hospital. As he regained consciousness he looked up through glazed eyes and said to his mother, "I told you it would happen, but you would not believe me, would you?" He still wonders to this day how he knew.

The second incident to occur, a few years later, was while he was living with his parents in Saudi Arabia. From time to time, when he was bored, Mark would wander out into the searing heat of the desert to collect scorpions and beetles.

One hot stifling day as he was doing this, he came across an old newspaper lying in the sand. He knew from past experience that he must use extreme caution in lifting the paper, as there was likely to be some form of life beneath it sheltering from the merciless rays of the scorching hot sun.

As he crouched down and reached forward, his hackles rose when he sensed an aura of impending death. In one swift agile movement he flung himself to one side and quickly rolled over as far as he could from the newspaper. On doing so, a huge snake that had been coiled in its protective shade, suddenly sprang out at him and shot over his shoulder, landing with a soft thud in the sand behind him.

If Mark had remained in the same position that he had been in only a few seconds earlier, crouching beside the newspaper, the snake would have caught him full on in the face, and as he was alone, he would have most certainly died from its poisonous venom, for it was the most deadly in the region; the King Cobra.

The premonition that something was wrong, and his prompt action, saved his life. It also stopped him collecting insects.

Weird Happenings at Harrogate

Harrogate is a beautiful town set in North Yorkshire. It is famous for its spa waters, which are said to contain healing properties. In the early Victorian times, people flocked from all over the country to come and bathe in the famous sulphur baths, which were said to be a cure for rheumatism, arthritis and various other maladies.

The hotels were always filled with wealthy, elderly people, who stayed in luxurious accommodation awaiting their treatment. It is in one of these hotels that the lady in this story works. I met her one evening at a party that was being held there, and she told me about her experiences.

For Grace, living in shared accommodation was no joke, but when you are living in a place like Harrogate you have to expect to pay top rents and rates if you want a home of your own. She had been advertising for a flat in the area for months, stating the price that she could afford to pay. Responses to her advert only brought properties of an inferior nature.

One day, as Grace was sitting alone in her bed-sit, she began to day dream about the kind of place that she dearly wished for; something spacious near the town centre, clean and at a reasonable rent, with her own bathroom and kitchen.

In her mind she was already decorating it with pretty wallpaper and furniture, when suddenly the ringing of the telephone brought her thoughts back to reality.

Her caller was a lady answering her advert for a flat. The lady told her that it was on the top floor, third floor, quite roomy, with her own bathroom and kitchen. Also, if she wished to view she could come and see it whenever she was ready, to see if it met her requirements. There was no hurry; they could discuss the rent after she had seen the property. Grace was over the moon and arranged to go the next day.

The following day, after work, Grace arrived at the premises for the interview at 11.00am. Upon her arrival she was greeted by a friendly lady, who immediately took her upstairs and showed her around. Grace could hardly believe her eyes, it was the same flat that she had been day dreaming about, right down to the shape and sizes of the rooms.

The bedroom was large, so was the living room, and it was furnished. The bathroom was of a good size, and the kitchen had plenty of work space. Instinctively she knew what the rent would be, and so was not surprised when the lady told her. The landlady smiled and nodded knowingly, when Grace said she would take it. After drawing up the necessary agreements, Grace went back to her bed-sit and wrote out her resignation.

As soon as the time was up, she moved into her new home and was extremely happy, but after a little while strange things began to happen to her. Every so often Grace would catch a fleeting glimpse of something that darted about the room that was too fast for her to be able to catch in her clear line of vision. Then one evening after she had come home from work and was sitting alone on the settee with a cup of tea in her hand relaxing, the video machine caught her attention.

As she watched, the numbers on the clock were racing madly round. Grace stared at it and thought, 'Stupid thing. What's wrong with it?' Then she realised that it was not plugged in and that the machine needed electricity to make it work. Rushing over to it she pulled at all the wires, and then picked it up and shook it, but the numbers carried on racing round. Panicking, she screamed, "Oh, my god!" Grace raced around the flat with the video in her arms not knowing what to do with it.

At long last she managed to calm down and put the video in a place that she did not use, covering it up so that she would not have to look at it, and then rang the repair shop to ask for someone to come and fix it. After the engineer had arrived and checked the video thoroughly, he could not find any fault with the machine. It was in perfect working order.

It remains a mystery to this day. How could the clock and machine work when it was unplugged and not connected to the mains?

Shortly after this, another strange incident occurred. It was Christmas 1986 when Grace brought home a considerable amount of gifts. She took the shopping out of her bags and placed each item on the bed, arranging the gifts for her friends in one place and the gifts for her relatives in another.

Grace intended to gift-wrap them later that evening, before going into the kitchen to prepare her evening meal. When the food was ready, Grace took it into the lounge and sat down to watch television whilst she ate.

After the warm food and a glass of wine, Grace became sleepy and decided to go to bed. She looked at the clock; it was after 11.15pm, and she had forgotten about gift-wrapping the presents. She decided to do them the following morning, and picked them up. When she took hold of some of the garments Grace was surprised to find that they were sopping wet. "What's happened here?" Grace said to herself. "I don't believe it!" She looked up at the ceiling expecting to find a damp patch, but it was perfectly dry.

Grace brought a bowl from the kitchen and squeezed the wet garments over it, before placing them on the radiators to dry. Next, she examined the bed, but there was no sign of wetness on her covers, which were bone dry.

Shaking her head in disbelief, she thought, 'That's unusual. I wonder if it could have come from the window. But it can't have, the window is over at the other side of the bedroom, water could not have splashed that far over without wetting the carpet.'

All the same she checked the window and found it was tightly sealed. Nothing could have come through, not even a draught, and the curtains were closed. She was absolutely stumped. Grace is still asking herself to this day, "Where did the water come from?"

Shortly after the water incident, Grace was at home one evening resting for an hour, before attending a large conference at the hotel where she worked, and knew that she would be rushed off her feet for most of that night. She went into the lounge and lay down on the settee. The last thing that Grace remembered thinking was 'I feel different,' and slowly drifted off into a very unusual sleep.

On awakening, she became aware that she was floating close to the ceiling, and on looking down at her reclining form, saw that there were two bearded men dressed in long white robes standing beside her, one on either side of her head. It was a strangely wonderful feeling of weightlessness, not having to control her body, something else was doing it for her and she didn't have a care in the world.

Suddenly she felt herself gently floating down and as she slipped into her body lying there, she was conscious of the men saying something to her, but could not understand them. She then began to feel herself waking up and immediately felt revitalised. It was as if she had slept for days and was completely relaxed.

As Grace began to sit up, she thought, 'Oh, no, it must be twelve o'clock, I'm going to be late for work.' She jumped up and looked at the clock and was surprised to see that it was only eight-thirty. What had seemed like endless hours of sleep had only been two hours. She had never experienced anything like this before, and felt that she had undergone something rather weird but wonderful and was strangely elated by it.

Still in a daze, Grace went into the kitchen to make herself some coffee to help pull her round. But, as she did so, she stopped and gaped in astonishment at the floor. Literally, scattered everywhere were diamond shaped pieces of ice; big solid lumps, all in a perfect diamond shape. She stooped and picked one of them up, but it was not cold, nor did it dissolve in her hand. "Where on earth could they have come from?' It's a warm night in the middle of August!" Grace asked herself.

There was nothing to account for the strange phenomenon at all. Grace picked up all the pieces and put them in the sink, fully expecting them to melt away with the warmth, but they didn't. Instead, they began to fade away, leaving no sign that they had ever been there. Since then, on odd occasions while she has been sitting in the lounge, she has seen large, diamond-shaped objects floating by her, shimmering and sparkling, then slowly disappearing.

When I interviewed Grace that evening, I was aware of the shapes before she had even begun to tell me about them. There seemed to be about thirty of these objects, floating closely together. They all floated gently over to one particular corner of the room and then disappeared.

The Channel of Energy at the South Lodge Inn, Ripon

The South Lodge public house at Ripon was first built as a private residence for two women who were millionaires, each in their own right. Sadly throughout the years the property was sold and bought by various occupiers and at one time was converted into a casino. That was about forty years before the present licensee, Rory Quinn. Therefore, because of the many people, either residing or visiting there, the building has amassed and held onto their emotions for many years within its old walls, causing small amounts of psychic activity that often occurs within old buildings of this age.

The most unusual activity inside this property however, is the powerful channel of energy that runs directly from the cellar, straight through the building and up to the roof top.

This could be described as a portal which has lain dormant for many years, waiting to be regenerated by some form of energy. The form of energy responsible for regenerating it came through a group of people and an Ouija board.

I love Ripon, set in North Yorkshire. It is an ancient town full of character and charm. In its bygone days many of the properties there had thatched roofs, and in June 1688, one man attempted to burn down part of the town by creating fires on the doorsteps of certain houses. When one woman asked him to put out the fire he struck her over the head with a pair of bellows, and carried on with his fire raising. His attempt was foiled by the courageous action of James Turpin, who saved the town and all its dwellers.

This is but one of the many true documented accounts of Ripon's past historical characters. Let us not forget though, that today Ripon is famous for its markets and quality antique shops, and on the 16th February 1993, this was where I was heading. It was approaching lunch time as I was driving with my daughter Leslie, towards Ripon, where, on the outskirts of the town, we spotted the South Lodge public house and decided to have our lunch there.

As we entered the spacious lounge and approached the bar, I stopped opposite a table surrounded by plush red seating near a bay window, where I felt to my left hand side a numbing icy cold presence that had suddenly sprang out of nowhere and was attempting to immobilise me.

It all occurred so quickly that I was taken by surprise. I did, however happen to glance towards the bar, where Leslie was now standing reading the menu, and noted the barman's reaction was one of tension and unease. As he stood watching me, I knew full well that he was aware of what I was sensing in that particular area. I did not say anything to him when I walked over to the bar, where Leslie was ordering our meal. When it came, I told her what I had felt.

Although our surroundings were quite pleasant, we found that one corner of space was not as amicable as the rest of the dining area, even though we were not seated in it, and mentioned this to the waitress. She then informed the licensee, Mr Rory Quinn, who came over to sit with us and explain what had transpired there.

It appeared that some time ago, when the staff had finished work and the pub was closed, they had seated themselves in that particular area and made an Ouija board with cut out letters of the alphabet and a glass ashtray to spell out the messages. At the start they all found it good fun, but stopped using it as things began to turn nasty, when twice, the heavy glass ashtrays had floated above them and exploded in mid-air showering them with shards of glass. Unknown to them, they had unleashed some kind of demonic force that was beyond their capability of understanding; a force they had no control over.

From then on, strange inexplicable happenings began to occur. Cold and hot spots, either froze or sweltered customers standing in different parts of the pub. Rushes of cold air would sweep past the staff behind the bar and in the kitchens. Bar staff became afraid to go down into the cellars alone, for when they were down there the cellar door would shut or open of its own accord. They also heard other doors in the cellar opening and closing causing them to panic and run, as they knew full well that there was only one door down there.

When Rory does his rounds at night after closing he has found that one area of the cellar becomes warm that should not be. Also, in one of the bar rooms the temperature drops below freezing upon entering and then warms up again within minutes. When Nick the barman went into the gents' the toilet door opened as he reached out to push it open. At first he thought nothing of it, but when the toilet flushed in front of him he panicked, yanked the door open and raced into the bar to tell Rory what had happened.

Since then his staff will only enter the toilets, as with the cellar, so long as someone accompanies them. They refuse to go anywhere in the pub alone. I asked Rory if it would be possible to take a look around the building. He said he had no objection and we were free to go where we wished. However, when we entered the cellar we experienced a rapid succession of temperature changes that occurred at an alarming rate. The cause of this came from a force of energy that was raging from beneath the cellar floor where we were standing, that spiralled into the room above, directly beneath the seating area where the Ouija board had been used.

I asked Rory if there was another floor beneath the cellar, as I felt certain there was another level beneath us, also, if there were more rooms beneath the house, on the cellar level that had been filled in. He was unsure about the cellar levels below, but he was certain that other rooms on this level had, for some unknown reason, been filled in. This was shown on the deeds.

We left the cellar and investigated every room, and were surprised to find that throughout the building the same force of energy I had found in the cellar flowed all the way up in that one specific corner of the building to the roof. That one corner is a tremendous power point throughout the building. His two Border collie dogs will not venture into those corners, they will sit, however, staring for hours with their ears pricked up and alert, as if they are on guard against a threatening adversary. From time to time the dogs relax their vigil for a few moments, and then will bark ferociously at something, as if barring its path, before sitting back to carry on staring into that one particular area. It really is unusual.

The phenomenon we did experience happened while we were upstairs, leaving the conference room. From that room is a dark corridor, and at the time I was the first out, Rory close behind me and Leslie last. Rory had just switched off the conference room light and was talking to me when Leslie screamed. Upon turning, we saw a man's dismembered hairy arm, with a white shirt sleeve, rolled towards the elbow with its fingers outstretched, hovering over Leslie's left shoulder, which had turned the light back on!

Leslie's eyes bulged with fear as she stood rigid and asked in a whispered voice, "Shall I turn it off?" Rory and I looked at her, then at the arm, and as Leslie turned the light off again, the arm disappeared. Leslie panicked and raced passed us yelling all the way down the stairs, and was in the bar shaking from head to toe, where Rory told us things like that occurred there on many occasions.

Another exceptionally weird phenomenon is that, although there are no trees or bushes close to the property's windows there comes a sudden drop in temperature, and even though the place is well lit, the area appears dark. The moment this happens weird scratching sounds can be heard coming from the outside onto the panes of glass, causing Rory and the staff to back away, in the fear that some invisible creature with gigantic claws is trying to get inside. Over and over the horrendous grating noise starts at the top of the window and slowly makes its way down to the bottom, setting everyone's teeth and nerves on edge. The, it slowly dies away, before the temperature and lighting returns to normal.

By some strange coincidence, a party was held for a ninety year old lady at the South Lodge only a few months previously. The lady in question had been the Head Housekeeper there many years ago. She informed Rory, that even in her early years working there it was a queer place and haunted! At certain times she did not like working in some of the rooms, and would peek around the doors before entering.

I believe that due to the alterations over the years the building has lost some of its identity and characteristic features, whereupon the many long dead owners, visitors and gamblers have left part of themselves there, and some are upset by the many structural alterations that have been carried out.

Also, the bad forces of energy that have been building up over the many years that the property has absorbed, had broken free due to the Ouija board, thus causing an extremity of haunting. Nevertheless, the South Lodge has a warm friendly atmosphere and the staff are very pleasant.

If you decide to pay a visit, take a walk over to the windows at the left hand-side of the bar, and see if you can sense whatever is there. If you can't, then listen for the sounds of tapping and scratching at the windows. You might just get lucky and see whatever is out there!

The Haunted Cottage at Holmfirth
The Handbag

I often wonder if it is something to do with a person's birth sign, which seems to attract spirit or psychic phenomena. In the events of these happenings, the lady was born under the sign of Aquarius, like me and many other people in my book.

In 1970 the couple involved, Joyce and Viv Bottomly, found what they had been searching for. For a long time they had been looking for a house where they could go and relax away from the rush and push of the hectic business life that they led in Harrogate. The property they found was at Holmfirth. It was a lovely old stone building, over a hundred years old, and had been at one time a weaver's house, consisting of a three story building that was now in use as two houses.

It could be seen from the outside, where the old pulley had been situated up on the top floor, for the lifting of heavy bales of whatever materials had been necessary to the business. The big, open archway was now sealed up and so were all the windows up on the top floor. At the time, only one of the two adjoining houses was for sale, so they bought it and were extremely lucky, as within a few weeks they managed to acquire the other house also, thus allowing them to make it into a decent-sized building.

An architect was brought in who redesigned the whole of the structure, converting it into a big property. The whole of the top floor was sealed off as they had no use for that part of the building, and on completion to keep it in balance with the local area. They decided to name it R.....Cottage, after the road it was standing on.

When everything was completed by the autumn; the decorating was done and the whole of the two lower areas were carpeted and furnished, they moved in. Upon arriving, shortly after lunch time, they took their suitcases from the car and carried them upstairs.

Before the arduous task of unpacking, Viv came back down stairs and lit a fire in the lounge, and in no time at all the fire was roaring in the grate, sending out a warm and welcoming glow about the room. He then placed a small table in front of the two comfortable armchairs that were set on either side of the fire, while Joyce made a cup of tea and placed it on the table before them.

They sat quietly in their comfortable surroundings and relaxed by watching the flames dancing in the grate, then drank their tea before going upstairs to start the unpacking. It was not until Viv had lifted one of the suitcases onto the bed that he realised he had left the key for it on the table in the lounge. "Don't worry about it," Joyce said. "You unpack the light luggage and I'll go down and fetch the keys for you." She went down the stairs and opened the lounge door, but as she did so, she was surprised to see a man sitting in one of the large comfortable armchairs. Without thinking she began to apologise saying, "Oh, I am sorry, don't let me disturb you." Then she realised, "What am I talking about, I live here!" Upon hearing her voice the man slowly raised himself up from the chair, walked over to the fireplace and leant against it.

In those few still moments of the man standing gazing into the fire's glowing embers, Joyce managed to take a good look at him. He was very tall and thin and wore an open-necked white shirt with the sleeves rolled up to the elbows, and a pair of dark-coloured trousers. As she watched the stranger, she became aware of an unusual silence about the house. It was then she realised her visitor was a ghost. Strangely enough she was not afraid. On the contrary, she found the incident intriguing, and waited to see what may transpire from his presence.

Once more the man began to move in the same discernible manner, and with the darkness of the room behind him, and the blaze of bright dancing flames illuminating the room about him, the man cast an eerie light of systematic colours of radiance. As he turned and walked around the chair towards her, he suddenly disappeared. This was the beginning of many unusual and inexplicable happenings in that house.

Upstairs, two of the bedrooms had an adjoining door, so you had to go through the first bedroom to get to the second one. Joyce could never account for the discomfort she always felt whenever she walked through into that room.

At first it wasn't too bad, but as time went by, every time she entered it, she would feel an icy coldness sweeping all around her, enveloping her body until she was completely engulfed by a suffocating force of freezing energy. She would then turn and run from that room, slamming the door behind her. It got so bad that whenever she got undressed in the first room, she would have to close the door to the second, as she was constantly aware of an invisible wraith watching her.

On numerous occasions, when Joyce was alone in the cottage, the sound of clogs could be heard distinctly thumping about. Someone was walking around overhead on the top floor which was sealed off. It was to be heard quite clearly as the upper floor was made entirely of concrete. But, as soon as her husband came home, the noise would cease. It was as if it only wanted her to notice. Each time it happened she would tell Viv and he would go upstairs and listen for ages, but each time he would come back down saying, "I can't hear anything up there. Are you sure you heard it?"

One night, as they lay sleeping in bed Joyce was awoken by loud noises overhead. As she lay there listening in the darkness, she realised that it was again the sound of clogs above her, clomping from one side of the room to the other. She sat up and then shook her husband awake, and before he had time to argue she said, "Listen, now will you believe me? There are some people up there. I told you so." This time he could not dispute the fact that someone was moving about up top as he could hear them very clearly, and promised to do something about it the following day.

The next morning at breakfast they discussed the previous night's events and decided to open up the top floor of the cottage. A contractor was brought in and in no time at all a way through was quickly completed. They were surprised by what they found. Amidst a pile of old junk and rubbish they came across an officer's uniform that dated back to the First World War. When Joyce lifted it and shook it straight she found it was riddled with bullet holes, and then began to wonder. Could the uniform have belonged to her mysterious visitor by the fire, and if so, was he responsible for the mysterious footsteps overhead, trying to draw their attention to the attic where the uniform was found?

After the attic was cleared and ht uniform handed over to the proper authorities the footsteps ceased and she never saw the man again. Many small mysterious happenings were to occur in their home in the months that followed, and they began to tire of it all, and as they were spending less time there they decided to rent the property out as a holiday cottage.

A couple from Sweden were chosen from the advertisement that they had run in the local paper, who were coming to Huddersfield to do some mineral surveying. They did not stay long as the young man was being driven to distraction by the invisible being on the second floor. He said it was evil and he could not cope with it, and regretfully had to leave. Joyce had had enough. She did not want the property as they were too uncomfortable in it and finally sold it to her son.

A few years later Joyce was working in the Huddersfield area, which meant travelling from Harrogate and back every day, so her son asked if she would like to spend a few nights with him and his wife. Hesitantly she accepted, as it was a long distance to travel each day.

On her arrival he told her that he had prepared the spare bedroom for her. "Oh, no," she said, shocked at him offering her that room. "I'll sleep on the settee down here." He would not hear of it and insisted that she spend the night in that room. After a slight argument and coaxing she finally relented and went up to bed. She left the adjoining door slightly ajar and kept the light on all night. Joyce was absolutely terrified.

On the third night of her stay her son popped his head around the bedroom door and asked if she was alright, as the light was on well after midnight, which was unusual for his mother. She didn't dare tell him that she was afraid to turn the light off, and nearly died of fright when he did and closed the bedroom door. Perspiration soaked her body as she lay petrified in the darkness, huddled beneath the bedcovers. Her temperature soared, and in the end she had to put her arm out of bed trying to cool herself.

Within seconds of her doing so, something furry touched her hand, accompanied by a growl. Horrified, she drew her hand quickly beneath the covers and lay cringing, tense and rigid with fear.

The growl came again and again, until Joyce finally recognised the sound; it was her pet dog Pepi who had died a short time ago. He had come back to let her know that she was safe with him to guard and protect her. A great feeling of joy and relief surged through her, with the realisation of why her old pet was there. She put her hand back down again and felt his soft silky head beneath her fingers. As she spoke and stroked his soft furry body, her fears evaporated and she finally slipped into a deep relaxing sleep. The last two nights she spent in that room did not upset her. Perhaps she regained her confidence having been forced to face up to her fears, or, was it the certainty of knowing that she had protection given to her, with the spiritual return of her faithful little Maltese terrier?

This little dog played an important role in the next happening when he was still alive.

Joyce had a close friend named Elsie, who lived only a few doors away from her in Leeds. One day, while they were holidaying in Bournemouth, the conversation turned to death and the return from spirit. At that time Elsie knew that she was about to die from cancer and had kept the knowledge a secret from everyone, even her own family. So it came as a surprise to Joyce when Elsie said, "If I die before you, I'll come back and let you know if there is a spirit world." Joyce could hardly believe what she was hearing, as her friend had never spoken to her like this before, and light-heartedly said, "Oh, yes, and how will you let me know that you are there?"

"I shall move something in the house," replied Elsie, and they both laughed.

Joyce leaned over and put her hand on her friend's arm saying, "You know what my husband is like, he's always moving things about, so I won't know any difference." Elsie thought for a moment and then said, "Do you remember when you had your bag stolen?" Joyce nodded. "Well, after that you said that you would never let it out of your sight again, and since that day you have never left it. It's always under your arm. I shall move your handbag!" Joyce laughed thinking that Elsie was joking, and it came as a shock to her the following year when Elsie died. Joyce was inconsolable. She had lost her closest friend.

Something strange occurred however; exactly a year to the day of Elsie's passing. Joyce was about to leave the house when the telephone rang, and putting her bag on the table she answered it. It was her daughter. As she was speaking her old dog, Pepi, began to growl and bark ferociously and within seconds he appeared to be attacking and snapping at someone's ankles beneath the table. Concerned, Joyce put down the phone and tried to console her agitated pet, but he would have none of it. He became hysterical; his fur stood on end and was sticking out at peculiar angles. With fangs bared and snarling, he began leaping up towards the table top yapping as hard as he could. Joyce could not believe it; her dog had never carried on like this before. Gradually he began to calm down, and with the occasional warning growl he allowed Joyce to lift and pet him, before slipping on his lead to go for a walk. In the midst of all the commotion she had never left the table, but when she reached for her handbag it was gone.

For three quarters of an hour she searched high and low for it. In the end she gave up, having gone through every room in the house. Feeling rather irritated she walked back in the kitchen and was astounded to see, directly in front of her was her handbag! It was placed exactly where she had left it earlier, in the centre of the table. There was no way she could have missed seeing it as it was so big and bulky. The bag had, for a period of time, disappeared.

At first Joyce did not connect the incident with her friend

Elsie who had died, but that evening after her husband, Viv, had taken the dog for a walk, a deathly hush had descended upon the house, and it was then Joyce realised what had happened. Elsie was there with her, she had moved the bag in the afternoon, and because Joyce had put the conversation made over a year ago out of her mind, Elsie had come back to remind her.

Elsie had said, "If there is another side of life, I will come back and prove it to you. I will move your handbag!"

Searching for Mother

When a young teenage girl became seriously ill, it affected her mind causing her to become child-like and completely dependent upon her mother. Wherever her mother went, Sylvia followed her around, hardly ever letting her out of her sight. However, within a couple of years the illness returned and became much worse than before, and the poor girl passed away.

Her heartbroken mother could no longer stand being in the house without her daughter. It held too many sad memories for her and she moved away, But the girl refused to leave the home where she had been so happy, and her soul could find no peace, therefore causing her spirit to haunt whoever lived there, and she was often seen flitting about in a disorientated fashion from one room to another, apparently searching for her mother.

On her first visit to look over the large terraced house in a secluded area of Pudsey, Bernadette fell in love with it. As she stood in the entrance hall a wonderful sensation of peace enshrouded her, and she knew straight away that this was meant to be her home.

Without appearing too eager, Bernadette managed to reach an agreeable price for the property, and in a matter of weeks the house was hers and she had settled in. Each day as she returned home from work, Bernadette always had time to spend a few moments with her neighbours and exchange a few pleasantries of the day, before going into her own home.

Once inside she would put on her comfortable slippers and prepare her evening meal, and then sit and watch television in the lounge. Situated in the lounge was a heavy, Victorian wooden door that contained in its upper portion, a large etched glass panel, enabling a view of the lounge, or hallway, from whichever area you were standing in.

One evening, as Bernadette was seated in the lounge, with her feet up watching her favourite television programme, she had a distinct feeling that someone was watching her. All of the curtains were shut, it was impossible for anyone to see in, so she excluded that possibility from her mind, and all the doors were locked, she knew that there could not be another person in the house.

Looking about she could find nothing out of the ordinary, and it wasn't until she had turned completely around that she saw the pale ghostly face of a girl peering at her through the glass panel in the door. Thinking that it was a reflection from the television, she turned and continued watching the programme, but the strange feeling of being watched persisted.

Once again she turned to look behind her, and saw to her amazement the same ghostly face peering intently at her that had been watching her only minutes ago. For a few fleeting moments their eyes locked as if held in surprise at what each other was seeing. The girl then turned her face and began to peer intently around the room, her eyes darting to and fro, as if searching for someone who she could recognise.

Concerned, Bernadette jumped up and rushed across the room, wondering how on earth this strange girl could have got inside the house without her being aware of it. By the time she had reached the door the face had disappeared. Outside in the hallway, Bernadette made a thorough check of the house only to find that she was quite alone and there were no signs of a forced entry.

Satisfied that no one was there, Bernadette realised that what she had seen was the ghost of a girl, and decided that on the coming weekend she would make a few discreet enquiries about the people who had lived there before her. With time to spare at the weekend she spoke to some of her neighbours who had lived in the area for many years, and asked if they knew anything of the past history of the house. They replied, "Yes, a little. Why, is something wrong, has something happened?" Bernadette related the past night's occurrences, telling them what she had seen. "Ah, that will be Margaret Shewit," said one of them. "Who was that?" Bernadette enquired.

"Well," said one of the elderly ladies, "there used to be a family living there, and they had a daughter that took ill in her teens. She couldn't bear to let her mother out of her sight, and followed her everywhere until she died. That's probably who you have seen. That will be Margaret Shewit looking for her mother."

Regardless of what she had just learned, Bernadette was not too disturbed about having a ghost in her home; in fact she was quite pleased.

From that day on, whenever Bernadette was either working or resting in the house, for no apparent reason doors would open and close of their own accord, and from the cellar sounds would echo up the stairs of coal being thrown into metal buckets. She could also sense the girl's presence most strongly in the back upstairs bedroom, and also had the distinct feeling that the girl was either watching her or following her about the house. Even so, she never felt afraid as Bernadette knew that the girl was quite harmless.

Perhaps the young ghost had taken a liking to her, as Bernadette would often sit in her quiet moments and find time to talk to her. She also, unknown to Bernadette, may have been taking care of Bernadette's health, for while Bernadette lived in that house she told me that she had never ailed anything, and that she was never so happy living in any other house as she was living there!

The Smell of Death

On occasions some of us can be pre-warned of the approaching death of a family member or a friend. It can come in the form of an apparition, knockings in the home, or an odour.

It was an unpleasant odour that stirred this man's memory, and he immediately knew that a member of his family was about to die.

The Christmas period brings both happy and sad memories for David, as he recalls an incident when he was a young boy of seven, which was to bring a forewarning of death ten years later.

He was living at the time in an area near Birmingham with his parents and grandma; the latter he thought the world of, and was greatly saddened when she died that Christmas.

As it was the holiday period there were no burial services, and her body had to be kept in the front room of the house for a number of days without any heating. Everything was alright at first, but after a few days, whenever he went into the room a peculiar rank odour would assail his nostrils that he did not like and could not understand.

Ten years later at the age of seventeen he was to experience the same odour again. It happened one day when

David arrived home from work earlier than usual and unlocked the front door. As he opened it, he recoiled and gasped for air as the same revolting stench hit him smack in the face, filling his nostrils and making him want to retch as it slowly wafted past him. David leant against the wall nauseated, feeling as if he was reliving the past experience of his grandmother's death all over again. Pulling himself together he took a few deep breaths before facing the house again, and forced himself to go inside.

David was absolutely terrified as he approached the door to the front room, and stood for a moment or two before gathering enough courage to open it.

His hands were shaking as he reached out and took hold of the door handle, and opened the door slowly, ready at any second to slam it shut again, for he fully expected to see his grandmother's body lying there.

Cautiously David peered in and let out a great sigh of relief when he saw that the room was empty, the curtains open and daylight was streaming in. Satisfied that everything was alright he closed the door then went into the kitchen and made himself a cup of tea while he waited for his parents to come home.

Upon their arrival, he told them of what he had experienced and asked if anyone was ill in the family, as what had happened was causing him concern. His parents told him not to worry, as far as they knew everyone in the family was fit and well. But he could not rest. David knew that someone was about to die.

Early the following morning a family awoke them with sad

news; a Great Uncle, his grandmother's brother, had died unexpectedly of a heart attack, and as his death had not been due to illness, it came as a great shock to the family.

David feels that his grandmother was trying to tell him that someone in the family was about to die, and the only way she could let him know was with THE SMELL OF DEATH.

Dinner at Twelve

More often than we care for, our lives are rules by time. Even when we die, for some of us this habit is hard to break. Like the elderly man in this story, who had died only days previously. He still arrived on a Sunday at 11.00am for dinner at twelve.

When Harry Livesy, from Wakefield, was a young boy he used tom live at Mill Hill, Blackburn. His grandfather lived only two houses down the street with his daughter at number 11. Every Sunday the whole family used to get together in the traditional British style, for their Sunday lunch of Yorkshire puddings and roast beef.

They always knew what time their grandfather would arrive, it would be spot on eleven o'clock, not one minute before or after. It was a sad day when the old gentleman died. Everyone felt that it would not be the same on a Sunday without him sitting there talking of the past and bringing back happy memories to each one of them. Yes, he was to be sorely missed. Then a strange thing was to happen.

It occurred only a couple of weeks after his passing, when the whole family had got together on the Sunday. As they sat talking in the front room, they heard footsteps walk past the front of the house, and then stop. Harry's mother waited for a knock at the front door, but there was nothing. It dropped deathly quiet in the house. No one spoke, and then they heard the front door open and then close, followed by footsteps entering and stopping at the vestibule door. This too opened and closed. Next, the footsteps approached the lounge door. The tension in the room was electrifying, as everyone there recognised the sound. It was their dead father returning.

With pounding hearts they all sat and stared watching the door, fearful of what may come through, as it slowly opened wide before silently closing.

The footsteps padded by them, closely followed by a draught of unnatural cold air that penetrated the bodies of each person seated there.

It was Harry's father who broke the stunned silence, as he stood with his watch in his hand and said in a shaky voice, "It is precisely eleven o'clock. Dad has come for his dinner!" The phenomenon was to occur for exactly four months, before it stopped. The old gentleman had not wanted to break his family ties. He wanted to be there with them and he was letting them know in the only way he could, by turning up at the usual time. They remembered him saying, "I shall be there at eleven, for dinner at twelve."

A Loving Touch at Evening

During the Second World War big cities and districts that contained large factories and naval bases throughout Great Britain were in constant danger from the barrage of bombs that were being dropped from enemy aircraft.

The Government realised what great danger they had put our children in and appealed to parents for the youngsters to be sent away to the safety of rural areas. One girl was lucky as she had relatives that owned a large house near Lincolnshire, and agreed to go and stay there on condition that her friend Irene went with her too.

It was here that both girls were to experience a gentle phenomenon, and, for Irene, it showed that although they were living in a cruel, bitter world, there was still so much love that did not end with death. That love came to her from the other side of life with a loving touch at evening.

Upon their arrival, Irene stared open-mouthed at the magnificent building before her. The house was enormous. It stood in its own vast acreage of well stocked gardens and woodland, and what added to its grandiose structure were the imposing bay windows with their stone turrets escalating above them. The doors that opened to welcome her were of thick solid oak, a sturdy but plain piece of craftsmanship in comparison with the rest of the house.

Inside was a high entrance hall and sweeping down into it was a magnificent oak staircase with a heavy carved balustrade and handrail. Along the hallway were doors leading to individual rooms, whilst those furthest away led to the kitchens.

After Irene had been introduced, the girls were given a torch each, but told to only use them after curfew, and to keep the blinds closed when the lights were on. They were then shown upstairs to the room they were sharing and asked to unpack before coming down to tea.

As Irene folded her belongings neatly away in the large chest of drawers the older girl asked her if she liked the house. "Well, it's a bit different to what I'm used to, but I do like it even if it is a bit posh," she answered. Her friend smiled and lowered her head, then her shoulders stiffened when Irene said, "There is something strange about it though. Since we came up the stairs I have felt as if someone was watching me. Can you feel it?" she asked. The older girl nodded her head, "It's years since I came here, but I always had that feeling." She glanced nervously around the room.

"Come on, let's go downstairs, I don't like it up here."

The days slipped into weeks and the girls became more relaxed in their surroundings, also with the aunt and uncle who were very kind and had accepted Irene as part of the family. They had fallen into a regular routine of meals, school, and, each evening before bed, of drawing the blackout blinds. But, although everything seemed normal in the house the girls noticed a disquieting strangeness about it.

Sometimes, as they were walking about the house, something would pass by them too quickly to be seen, but slow enough to be noticed, and at various times they would experience abnormal changes of temperature.

It was never unpleasant, but slightly unnerving as the girls were young and didn't quite understand what was happening. One night, after supper the eldest girl witnessed something that scared her half to death. Seeing as the moon was shining brightly when the girls went to bed, they decided to open the blinds and allow the moon's silver-blue rays to penetrate the darkness, thus dispersing light about the gloomy old room and directly onto the bed where the two girls lay talking before settling down and falling asleep.

The elder girl had only slept for a short while, when something compelled her to awaken. Upon opening her eyes she saw illuminated eerily in a shaft of glimmering moonlight, the phantom figure of a Victorian lady bending over Irene and gazing into her face. A scream entered her throat as she tried to reach over and touch her friend to warn her, but the scream never emitted from her throat for she found herself speechless and paralysed. She could only look on in awe as the phantom lady began to tuck in the loose covers about Irene's still form, and then with a tender, loving touch, began to stroke her head, speaking silently to her.

After a short while, she straightened up and stood looking down at Irene, before turning and walking over to the dressing table. She paused for a moment as if she had forgotten something, then came back and touched Irene again. Terrified, the girl watched as the phantom slowly walked back to the dressing table and disappeared into it. At that precise moment she found herself free from the restricting force that held her and shook Irene awake.

Sobbing with fright, she told her what she had just witnessed, and within seconds Irene was sat bolt upright, her nerves all a-jangle as she grabbed her torch and hastily shone its beam around the bedroom and saw that no one was standing by the dressing table. Terrified, the two girls clung to each other for the rest of the night, too afraid to close their eyes in fear that the phantom should reappear.

When morning came the girls hurriedly dressed and went down to breakfast. The aunt noticed that they were subdued and quiet and asked if they were alright. The girls looked at each other before the elder girl said, "Aunty, I think this house is haunted," and went on to reveal the previous night's events. "Oh, dear, I suppose I shall have to tell you now," her aunt replied. "Yes, this house is haunted. I did not want to say anything about the ghost, as I knew you would have been afraid. Many people have seen her; it's the lady who lived here many years ago. Your uncle and I have often seen her. She comes from the kitchen into the dining room here, and sits for a while at the table. Then after a while she rises and walks through the door into the hallway and up the stairs. We have tried to follow her, but she disappears by the time we get to the landing. Many times, when we are sitting quietly in the lounge, we can hear the clicking of her knitting needles by the fire. Speaking of your experience, some of the guests who have slept in the room that you two are occupying tell the same story as you."

"So, I was not having a bad dream after all, I knew it was happening," the older girl said defensively. "Although it scared me, I feel better now that you've told us. Now I can eat my breakfast."

Although the girls were afraid and uneasy knowing about the ghost, they realised that it would not harm them. Even with their partial acceptance of it, they found that whenever they detected any unusual sounds or movements coming from the rooms, they were afraid to enter, and suffered many anxious moments during their stay at Grantham.

Irene had, at first enjoyed living in the big house in the country, but after what she and her friend experienced, she said that she would never go back to it as it was a very strange house!

The Face at the Window

Cornwall is a beautiful part of England, and it is here where thousands of tourists flock to in the summer season to visit the vast, open countryside or go walking on the pleasant golden beaches and investigate the caves and coves. It was in Falmouth, Cornwall that a young couple, Leanne and David from Wakefield went to live for a short while due to David's work.

At the back of the shop where they were living, a four-story high extension had been built, and they occupied the top flat on Market Strand. One evening as they were sat talking, David mentioned that he had not been in touch with his Uncle Jim up in Scotland for a while. The last letter he had received from one of his relations stated that the old man had not been too well, so David decided to write to him. He posted the letter the following morning as he went off to work.

Something unusual was to happen a few days later, however, and it was in the early hours of the morning that David awoke with a start. He shook Leanne awake, "look!" he said, pointing to the window facing them. She rubbed her eyes and gazed sleepily towards the window and then shrieked, "oh, my god, what is it?" There was an old man's face staring in at them from the outside. David said to her calmly, "don't be afraid, that's my Uncle Jim. He's come to see me." She promptly replied, "don't talk silly, it can't be him he's too poorly to travel, and anyway, we're four floors up." Her flesh crept as she realised what she had just said and held onto David.

The face stayed there gazing in at them for a few moments longer, then slowly faded away. Leanne was extremely frightened by this strange happening, but David was not. He took it as some kind of omen.

The following day his mother rang from the Midlands telling him that his Uncle Jim had passed away in the early hours of the morning. She could hardly believe her ears when her son told her that both he and Leanne had witnessed his Uncle's face at the window. David believed that the old man had come to see him, either before passing over, or immediately after, knowing that his nephew believed in life after death.

The Weird Mansion

This is a story about three sisters, Doreen, Mary and Sharon. Doreen and Mary share their belief of the supernatural and have experienced precognitive dreams and see apparitions, while Sharon, the youngest sister, was a non-believer who changed her mind after a hair-raising experience in the weird mansion.

From the very first moment of experiencing the awe inspiring dream, Doreen knew that it held a significant meaning for her and her family. After a strenuous day's work in the fish and chip shop in Old Town, Bridlington, which she and her husband Brian owned, Doreen was only too pleased to shut up shop, go home and step into a hot foaming bath, where she would relax and release the stress that had built up throughout the day, before sliding into bed.

The moment her head touched the pillow she was fast asleep and dreaming, where she found herself standing on a well-kept lawn gazing up at the stone walled structure of a seventeenth century country mansion. In the next instance she was launched inside the building, where she was standing in a long stone corridor that had two fairly steep stone staircases at either end of it, leading up into darkness. At that moment Doreen felt that something was very wrong and an unprecedented danger was lurking close by. All at once she found herself asphyxiating and forced herself to awaken from her hidden terror, and sat up to calm herself before dozing off again.

The dream had alarmed Doreen to such a degree that she told Brian about it at breakfast, who said nothing to calm her fears except not to worry about it.

A few nights later however, she had the same dream again, only this time she walked along the gloomy corridor which had many rooms on either side of it. As she walked along, Doreen felt a strong compulsion to enter one of the rooms, and stopped to open the door, where she was surprised to see her sister Mary standing there. Instinct told her that Mary was in imminent danger and that something bad was about to befall her.

She had to get out of that room. Without hesitation, Doreen rushed into the room, grabbed her sister by the shoulders and dragged her forcibly out of the room and the building to safety. The next thing Doreen became aware of was that she was awake in her own bed, perspiring and trembling with the intensity of the dream. This time she awoke Brian and told him, otherwise she would never have slept that night.

A few weeks later Doreen decided to visit her mother who lived in Lincolnshire. On her arrival she was greeted by her mother and sister Mary, who went into the kitchen to make a pot of tea. Thus Doreen found that it was a good opportunity to tell her mum about the disturbing dreams. Upon doing so, she watched her mother's face slowly pale, "Don't say anything of this to Mary when she comes in, will you?"

Surprised by her mum's reaction, she shook her head, saying, "No, not if you don't want me to. But, why should I not tell her?" Doreen asked.

"It's because of something that happened a short while ago. Wait until she comes back and she'll tell you."

The cups rattled on their saucers as Mary carried the tray through into the lounge, and placed it on the table before sitting down to pour the tea. "Mary, tell Doreen what happened to you and Sharon when you both went on holiday," her mother said.

"Oh, god, it was horrible, it makes me shiver just thinking about it. You should have been there, Doreen, it was weird. It happened while we were down south, when Sharon and I decided to visit an old country mansion house. It was a massive old stone building, beautiful to look at, but something was wrong with it. I couldn't say what it was, but it unnerved me. As soon as we reached the door my instincts were telling me to run. In fact, I very nearly didn't go in. It was only because of Sharon that I went inside at all. Anyway, you know what we're like, once inside we went our separate ways. Sharon went upstairs, and I decided to look around the lower floors. At first everything was alright, it was spacious and airy, some of the floors were carpeted and others were polished floor boards or marble mosaic designs that I found very impressive.

"What I did find strange though was that after going down a narrow stone staircase and through an archway, I found myself standing on a flagged floor in the centre of a long stone walled corridor. To either side of me was a wide stone staircase leading upwards into the semi-darkness. Straight in front of me were big stone arches, and I couldn't help wondering if the open area there had been either the old kitchen cellars, or worse, the dungeons. It was extremely creepy and cold. Maybe it was the stone surrounding me or the musty smell, but whatever it was; I didn't like it there, and went back the way I came.

"Regardless of my unease, after wandering around various rooms, I did enjoy seeing the fine antique furniture, especially in one room. I was so taken with everything, that I didn't notice a cold chill sweeping into the room. When I did, however, it was too late, for the very second that I felt it, for some unimaginable reason I couldn't move and knew I was in terrible danger. The feeling of helplessness was so intense, I thought I would pass out, when suddenly I felt a pair of hands drop onto my shoulders that began to push me out of the room. As soon as I was out I just screamed and ran outside, getting as far away as possible from the building as I could.

"This will sound stupid, but as soon as I could move I turned my head to see who was behind me, yet no one was there, even so, the weight of the hands were still on my shoulders until I was outside the building. No matter who or what pushed me out of there, I am thankful to it, for it certainly saved my sanity".

Sharon

Meanwhile, Sharon, who had begun on the top floors, had eventually reached the lower regions of the house, and was now standing in the centre of what she believed to be the cellars. From where she could see in the semi-darkness, there were two identical stone staircases leading down onto the cobbled stone floor where she now stood. What she did find unusual was that there were three entrances and exits into that one vast area, all situated in one place. She had entered the cellar through an arched doorway between two staircases. Sharon thought this intriguing, and became so engrossed trying to fathom it out, she didn't notice the temperature dropping about her.

When she did however, it was too late, for as she turned, she saw sweeping directly towards her a light mist, which turned into a thick fog as it settled all about her completely cutting out any light that was to be seen. Sharon gasped with shock, disbelieving the speed of the fog's momentum as it twisted and twirled about her. In the next instance however, it stopped and in one area began to slowly break down, where she saw a strange shape emerging.

At first she could not recognise any discernable features, but as the mist cleared she found herself confronted by a man with a horribly deformed face, who stared in an intimidating manner into her eyes. In the same instance she felt two hands drop onto her shoulders that propelled her away from the terrifying person standing there. Immediately the hands had touched her she screamed incessantly, which must have affected the man, for as soon as Sharon had screamed, both he and the fog rapidly disintegrated.

The moment he disappeared the hands lifted from her. She was free. In sheer blind terror she turned and ran from the building, as if the very devil was after her. It was an experience never to be forgotten.

It was strange how Doreen had the two dreams of the same country mansion; the first dream with the identical stone staircases leading from one room, and the second dream of rescuing her sisters from unseen danger, before her two sisters had their experiences, in the same building at the same time. Can our dreams be foretellers of the future? We often wonder. Who knows?

The Holy Island Ghost

Mr Smith never thought for a moment that he could possibly have photographed a ghost, when he was taking pictures of a church window.

However, after extensive examinations, it appears that he has caught something not of this world in his pictures.

In 1996 I happened to speak to a young woman who was interested in my investigations into the paranormal. She told me about an unusual photograph that her father had in his possession that he had taken in 1978, when he had visited a church on the Holy Island, Northumberland.

He had gone there specifically to photograph the church windows, as he takes a great deal of interest in antique stained glass artefacts.

Due to the fact that there was only a couple of people in the church at the time, and no one in the aisle before him, he thought as it was so quiet he would take a couple of photographs, and proceeded to photograph the stained glass windows and the church interior.

There had been no one in the aisle either before or after the photograph was taken. However, when the photos were developed he was surprised to find a man walking directly towards him. In fact, he was almost on top of him. His daughter said, "to this day my father swears there was no person walking down the aisle. The reason he took the picture was for the window, and, furthermore, what reason could he have to take the photo of a complete stranger? None whatsoever."

She kindly offered to give me the picture for my investigations. In due course she sent me the negative and I had it developed.

In the centre aisle was a man walking towards the camera, his head and the top part of his right arm transparent. The rest of his body 'appears' solid. At first glance I had thought, like her father, that the blurring on the negative was due to a double exposure, but when developed it appeared quite different.

I took it to the National Museum of Photography, Film and Television at Bradford, where I left it for Paul Thompson to investigate and give me a written report. Upon examination after six weeks and its return, Mr Thompson informed me that he had searched for many reasons why the man should have appeared looking as he did, when there was no one in the aisle at the time the photograph was taken. He admitted that it was a puzzler. The only other explanation he could offer was that Mr Smith had photographed a ghost!

With no one else in the aisle, where did this headless body come from?

Bill, where are you?

The latter stages of pregnancy can be very tiresome for almost every mother to be, even more so for Sally Hudson who, in her eighth month was expecting twins.

To make matters worse was the fact, that whenever she wanted to travel anywhere she had to rely upon her husband Bill, on account of her protruding bump that had made it impossible for her to drive at all; she could not fit behind the steering wheel. Therefore, every night she enjoyed a run out to the factory where Bill, who was the foreman, had to go and check that the night shift workers had no problems.

As the factory was on the Pontefract Road and not too far away from their home, they always took their Dalmation dog, Mandy, along as company and protection for Sally as she strolled around the open grounds and nearby scrubland while waiting for Bill to finish his rounds.

On this particular night, in 1968, they arrived at the factory at about 10pm, where Bill went inside, leaving Sally to take the dog for a walk around the field close by some derelict buildings that belonged to the company.

The dog would always romp about, then race back again to Sally's side for a fuss, and then would be off again. The dog, however, on this particular night appeared uneasy and over protective towards Sally and never left her side. At first Sally thought she must be having a mood and tried to get Mandy to go for a run. But the dog was having none of it and sidled up to Sally, who nearly fell over her a few times.

Sally was even more perplexed when Mandy began to bark up at the sky in a strange screeching manner before throwing her head back and letting out a spine chilling howl, and then shot off into the darkness. In her condition, Sally could not run after Mandy, but stood calling her name. At first she was more concerned than angry about the dog's strange behaviour, and knew that Mandy must have been really frightened to have run off like that. Yet as Sally looked up above and about her, there was nothing to be afraid of.

With the moon being at its peak, Sally could make out all of the shapes recognisable to her, therefore was not too concerned about being alone in the dark, and set about walking towards the bushes into which Mandy had fled.

She was so engrossed in searching for the dog that she failed to observe an object of unwieldy size that was moving above her. When she did, however, look up, to her amazement she saw a silver circular craft of immense proportion hovering there. Furthermore, to make matters worse, she found herself caught up in its spasmodic bursts of glaring light, and was unable to move. "Oh, god, this can't be happening to me. It's not real. Bill, where are you?"

As luck would have it at that precise moment Bill had left the factory and was walking over in her direction, when he had seen the craft unexpectedly appear out of nowhere, which was now hovering above his expectant wife, who was standing directly beneath the craft, silhouetted and encased in its hypnotic flashing white lights. For a few brief seconds, Bill was too shocked to move, and then the adrenalin took over.

He raced to Sally's side, and after grasping her in his arms, dragged her to safety into the protective area of a nearby derelict building

Breathless and unable to speak, they leant against the wall shivering more from fear than the chilly night, until they had recovered enough energy to make their way over the piles of rubble towards one of the shattered windows, where they watched and noted that it appeared to look like a domed saucer with many windows, and from the extreme centre a pulsating white light flashed on and off. They were unable to define its size as it was so big.

It seemed like forever before the craft finally, without sound, zoomed away into the night sky at an incredible speed, until it was only a pinpoint of light. Thankful that it had gone, they made their way outside, and were relieved to see Mandy returning, safe but scared to death, whimpering with her tail between her legs. Bill admitted that he was scared, but his main concern had been for Sally and the babies. They both agreed that for the amount of time they had spent in its glaring lights and also hidden, they felt as if they were being scrutinised by an unknown force aboard the vessel.

Not very long after the sighting Sally went into labour and was haemorrhaging badly. She was rushed to Leeds General Infirmary, and as the ambulance raced to the hospital, Sally felt the life drain out of her, and began spiralling downwards into a deep black hole while losing consciousness. All of a sudden the fall began to reverse itself and she was drawn towards a comfortable white light. Sally became aware that she was floating above herself, watching a team of doctors working frantically over her still, prostrate body as they fought to save her life.

All of a sudden she felt an overwhelming necessity to return, and awoke with an over anxious medical team gazing down at her, breathing an immense sigh of relief. It was not until a few hours later that they told her they had nearly lost her, and the sad news that one of her babies had died. Sally and Bill can't say for certain if it was the UFO experience that had caused the sudden premature births. They didn't, however, discard the idea from their minds.

Dead Creepy

Hazel Mills never dreamed that one day she would be haunted by the ghost of a young girl, when she and her husband John took over a shop in the Thornton Arcade, Leeds City centre. When they first moved in they noticed that the shop upstairs was boarded up and not let out to anyone. At the time Hazel thought it was a little odd as the shop appeared to be of a good size and it seemed such a waste to leave it empty. But, as they were so busy settling in and setting on staff they never thought to ask the reason why.

At the start the business was competing very well with other stores selling similar products, and then for some obscure reason things began to go wrong.

Also, at the same time, a strange phenomenon began to occur, starting with a large metal post dropping from one of the racks onto the floor, and as they watched, was followed by boxes falling from the shelves when no one was nearby. At first Hazel wondered if it could have been caused by the vibration of the traffic, but quickly dispelled the idea as that particular zone of road was partially pedestrianised, plus that area was a good distance away from her shop, in fact, they could find no justifiable explanation as to what was happening there.

The next thing to happen was that the staff began to leave as they were afraid when the phenomenon carried on late at night as they restocked the shelves and did the cleaning. Every so often, to everyone's relief, the phenomenon would stop and everything would revert back to normal. Nevertheless, within a few weeks it would return with a vengeance and set their nerves on edge.

Then another anomaly started to occur, when they went upstairs to use the toilets and washrooms they had to pass the boarded up shop, and as soon as they approached its door, cold gusts of wind would sweep by them, and cease when they were clear of it.

This created a great deal of anxiety amongst everyone, as they knew that the whole area upstairs was sealed off at both ends; there was only one way up and down, and was absolutely draft proof.

It was no use Hazel telling her staff not to be afraid as she was just as scared as they were. The girls started to go to the washrooms in pairs, and when Hazel found herself working alone late at night, she used other peoples' facilities. To give herself peace of mind, Hazel began asking customers and shop keepers if they knew anything about the boarded up room, and eventually discovered that many years ago a young girl had been burnt to death there and her restless spirit was rumoured to haunt that area. That was the reason why the room was boarded up.

Then she found out something else that was disturbing; the room the girl had died in was directly above Hazel's shop, and everyone who had taken it on had a run of bad luck. This upset Hazel, but she vowed to succeed with her business. Her efforts were being thrown into turmoil however, when she and the girls began to feel icy cold fingers touching the nape of their necks. The girls had had enough and left Hazel to carry on alone.

Hazel tried to carry on as normal, but found that her nerves were getting so bad that her health began to suffer. To make matters worse her husband told her that it was all a figment of her imagination and didn't believe her. He did have a change of heart however, after picking her up from work late one night. As they were driving home they were talking about the shop and began arguing about what was happening there, when, from out of nowhere a cold draft swept around the van before enveloping her neck. "She's here!" Hazel screamed. "Can't you feel the cold?"

"Don't be silly, it's your imagination that is playing tricks on you again," he sneered.

His flippant reply must have angered whoever was there; it retaliated by sending the temperature plummeting in the van.

"Now do you believe me," she shouted at him.

"No," he replied. "One of the van doors must have come open." Although he would not admit it, John was more afraid than Hazel, and jammed his foot down hard on the accelerator and raced home.

He tried all the doors, but they were locked. From that day on he never scoffed at what she said was happening in the shop, in fact, it helped him make up his mind to sell the business. Hazel said she would never step foot in those premises again. It was dead creepy.

The Haunting of Pearoyd Bridge - The Background

There are three incidents that could have led up to the haunting on Pearoyd Bridge at Stocksbridge, Sheffield, and the new by-pass below, during the construction of the A161 Liverpool to Skegness Road.

Two of the incidents were told to me by a local historian from Stocksbridge, and are on record, whereas the other is not recorded but is spoken of by the local people.

(Unrecorded)

During the mid-nineteenth century, amidst a heavy snow storm, a coach driver wearily urged his tired horses on. Another half a mile and they would arrive at Burton-Under-Edge coaching house the stopping place for weary horses and travellers.

Can you imagine the fear and horror as the coach began to slide on the perilous steep, twisting incline, which led to Pearoyd Lane? The driver fought to control the terrified, whinnying horses as they tried to regain their footing upon the icy stones and snow, but to no avail; they could not hold back the tremendous weight of the fully laden coach.

The brakes man tried to wedge the wheels to help the

panic-stricken animals, but it was no use. The coach began to slide sideways and then toppled over, dragging the horse and occupants along with it, screaming and shrieking down the hill. Baggage flew from its straps, landing at each side of the road, scattering the meagre belongings of the people, on the last disastrous journey they would ever make.

The coach slid over the frozen grass, hitting low stone walls, leaving wrecked timber and broken bloody bodies scattered over the hillsides, before coming to rest alongside the old Pearoyd Bridge. It is said that the remains of the people and horses were buried alongside the bridge where the tragedy occurred, and the coach remains were left to crumble and decay into the ground where it met its sad demise.

(Recorded)

John Ball Brown owned the Green Moor Stone Quarry and the Stage Coach Wagon Company. He used to take stone from his quarry down to Goole for shipment south to the River Thames. It was to be the last load of stone that John Ball Brown and his mates were ever going to carry, as they set out in the middle of a snow storm that was later to become a blizzard, on those wild, open moors.

When they reached the treacherous slopes of Don Hill and Pearoyd Lane, to get down to the village of Wortley, visibility was down to zero and the snow was deep, so deep in fact, that the horse misjudged the road and hit a low wall, thus causing them to fall and roll down the steep hillside, killing the driver and his mate.

The last coaches and wagons to travel along Langsett Road

were in May 1876. Burton-Under-Edge Farm on Don Hill used to be the resting place for all travellers. Drivers, with their coaches and wagons used to stop to recuperate and rest the animals before carrying on with their journeys. (Recorded)

John Dixon, who used to live at Tolebar House, Middock, was a coachman who used to ride up top alongside the driver, with his shotgun ready to protect his passengers from highwaymen. Times were very bleak in those days and theft was rife. After he died, a little ditty was written about him;

> *John Dixon the coachman*
> *No more shall be seen,*
> *Travelling from Sheffield*
> *To Fiddler's Green.*

I will leave it up to you, the reader, to decide for yourselves - who are the ghosts on Pearoyd Bridge?

The Haunting Of Pearoyd Bridge, Stocksbridge, Sheffield

In Mid-November 1987, my husband, Eric, arrived home with news of ghosts and mysterious happenings, which had been related to him by a farmer at Burton-Under-Edge, Stocksbridge. The man had told him about a haunting at his farm entrance, leading onto Pearoyd Bridge, where ghostly sightings and weird phenomena had been witnessed by security guards and police officers, both on the bridge and below, where the new A161 by-pass road was under construction. As I have an interest in the paranormal, Eric offered to take me out to the site, as he had to see the farmer again later that day.

I followed Eric in my own car with Leslie, our daughter, through Denby Dale and out onto the cold blustery moors. The roads that we turned onto were narrow and winding, but when we rounded the corner of Don Hill we were in for a shock. The road disappeared from sight as it veered treacherously down into a steep, twisting incline onto Pearoyd Bridge.

With a great deal of caution I drove steadily down the icy hill, and after parking the car at the side of the farm entrance we began to investigate, and made notes about the area. Before us, the beauty of the spacious moorland was marred by the sight of newly constructed pylons, carrying thousands of kilowatts of electricity for miles into the far distance.

In an instant we agreed that if there was a genuine haunting, then the constant flowing energy through the overhead cables could actually be helping the disturbed spirit to materialise. Bearing this in mind,

I photographed the bridge where the guards had seen the manifestations, and the road below, where the police had experienced phenomena. There was, however, a large amount of earth moving equipment and people working down there, so we could not go down.

The road-widening had meant digging into the surrounding hillside, and the arduous excavations had been aggravated by bad weather conditions, thus causing the banking below to be turned into a coagulated quagmire. Nevertheless, I decided that we should return that night while the phenomena was still occurring and delve into the mysterious manifestations.

Together we planned our safest path down knowing that the slope would be extremely dangerous when it was dark, before driving home to prepare for our long night's vigil.

At 10.15pm that night we set off for the sight and arrived at 11pm. I parked in the same position as I had done earlier that day, and turned off the lights. It was pitch black, no stars, no moonlight, just the wind howling eerily around us. We sat with the windows down for half an hour, watching in silence, yet there was nothing. The only activity on Pearoyd Bridge was coming from the traffic lights that changed when the occasional car went by. I decided it was time to take a look around.

As I opened the car door, and suggested to Leslie that we get changed into our walking boots and warm clothes to investigate the site, the traffic lights went berserk, changing in rapid succession from one colour to another. Ignoring the activity we put on our warm clothing, picked up our camera and torches and began to walk down the road. It wasn't until we reached the bridge however, that we felt the full extremities of the cold night, and I realised that I had only one glove in my pocket.

I told Leslie that I was going back to get my other glove, plus an extra scarf, whereupon we turned back up the road and returned to the car. We were only about three feet away from the car when we stopped and watched in fascination as the back door slowly opened of its own accord. "Well, here we go again," said Leslie, shuffling behind me. "You go and get the things and I'll wait here."

Undeterred, I walked up to the car, then drew back gasping for clean air as a fetid stench assailed my nostrils. At the same time I glanced down onto the back seat and was surprised to see my thick woollen scarf neatly folded with the black glove placed on top. The reason I found this odd was the fact that our outdoor clothing had been locked in the boot. Equally surprising was the car had a central locking system and it was virtually impossible for only one door to be opened while the rest remained locked.

Whatever had opened the door was close by as the stench had, by now, floated out of the car and was encircling me. With a swift movement I grabbed both scarf and glove, before slamming the door shut. I had to unlock the driver's door to re-lock the whole system.

For some reason my nerves felt jagged and I grabbed Leslie by the arm, dragging her down towards Pearoyd Bridge, and didn't stop until we reached the area where we could, in relative safety, stop to regain our breath.

Regardless of the incident, we proceeded to walk along the road past the disorientated traffic lights until we reached the area where we could climb down the embankment safely. The dark tendrils of the night closed all around us making it virtually impossible to see where we were treading as we carefully made our way down the steep slippery slope. Each step taken was heavy and laborious as the near-freezing sludge dragged and sucked at our feet when we sank to our ankles in the thick oozing mass. Using our torches we could see where the broken limestone began, that had been laid for the workmen to walk over, and made our way towards it.

It was also detectable in the beam of light where the ground disappeared into a vast abyss of emptiness. Undeterred, we made our way forward onto firmer ground. Whereupon it was at this point, in the dark heavy silence of the lonely night, surrounding us on the still desolate moors of Stocksbridge, that we heard footsteps crunching on the gravel behind us. With steady defined movements I motioned to Leslie to come to my side, which she did, and whispered, "Mum, can you hear someone following us?"

I nodded, saying, "when I say, now turn around and shine your torch at whoever it is. Are you ready?"

"Yes," she answered.

"Right, now!" We both turned. The brightness of our lights stood out in the inky blackness as we directed the beam at the oncoming footsteps, but no one was there, it was just an empty space.

We stood looking at one another. Leslie was mortified when the footsteps reached us, and then stopped. We waited for a while but nothing happened. Leslie reached for my hand and we both turned. Without any warning she received a tremendous blow to the centre of her back that pushed her roughly forwards, jerking her hand from mine. Within seconds, the breath was knocked from my body, as I received a blow that sent me staggering forwards.

I managed to grab hold of her as we were repeatedly pushed, my main concern being the steep drop down onto the dual carriageway ahead. However, the strange power seemed to know what it was doing, as simultaneously we were manoeuvred into a place where it wanted us to be and then stopped. We stood still, fully expecting something else to happen, luckily it didn't. But each time we tried to move away from that spot, invisible hands pushed us back. So, finally, we gave in and stayed put.

It took us a few moments to unwind from the tension that had built up within us, and were astonished to find ourselves in an area that was extremely warm, yet it was a freezing cold night. The wind that had been whistling about our ears had gone. Silence surrounded us. We stood still for a few moments and took stock of the situation, before I suggested that we move about and feel where the warmth ended and the cold began, and found that we were in a perfect, eight foot circle of heat.

I can't remember how long we stood there; it felt like 15-20 minutes discussing the strange phenomenon, when the temperature suddenly began to rise. We decided to move out. Cautiously, we stepped out of the circle ready to face our invisible assailant, but we need not have worried, it had gone and everything was back to normal.

Breathing a sigh of relief we moved away and, on looking back, we saw that we had been pushed into an area very close to being beneath the top arch of the bridge.

We searched closer to the edge of the slope, but declined from going any further as it was too dangerous to carry on. We had also begun to feel ill. So, we made our way back to the car.

After changing our boots and coats we then locked ourselves in the car and looked at the clock. It was after 3.00am. We couldn't believe it, so we turned on the radio.

Sure enough it was well after 3.00am. We had lost time in the circle of heat. To be honest we were quite shocked, nothing had ever happened to us like this before. To help us relax, Leslie poured us both a hot chocolate drink. I lowered the windows as they had begun to steam up, and we wanted a clear view all around us, in case something else happened.

We didn't have long to wait. Within half an hour the temperature dropped at an alarming rate, accompanied by a foul, putrid, unnatural smell that filtered unnoticed into the interior of the car. We gasped for breath as the oxygen was rapidly drawn from the air about us, causing our sense to reel. Instinct forced me to move, as a prickling numbness began to creep from my feet upwards. I reached out my left hand to the control switch and closed all the windows. As I did so, Leslie gasped, "Mum, look. What is it? It's at my side!"

I forced my head around and could see a figure dressed completely in black standing beside her. We both watched in silence, as it began to glide very slowly around the car, until it had completely encircled it, and then stopped for a few seconds beside Leslie, before disappearing. In no time at all our breathing was back to normal, the numbness had left our bodies and the coldness, along with the fetid odour had drifted away. Everything was back to normal.

My immediate reaction was to switch on the car headlights, grab a torch, leap out of the car and search about the area where the figure had been, but there was no sign of anything having been out there. When I got back into the car, Leslie was in no fit state to experience anymore, so I drove home.

Later that morning I rang the farmer and he told me the haunting experienced by the police and security guards had been published in the Sheffield Star. I contacted the newspaper, who obliged by sending me a copy of the published account.

From there, I contacted the security guard's boss, Mike Lee, and was informed that one of the men involved in the ghost scare had already left his employ. I did, however, ask the other guard if he would relate his experience to me and he agreed.

We arranged to meet on Pearoyd Bridge, but he never turned up. I think the strain of what he had undergone earlier had been too much for him.

Two weeks later, Leslie and I returned to Pearoyd Bridge. We investigated the area again and waited until the early hours of the morning, but all was quiet and peaceful. We did speak to the farmer's son though, who had come home late. He recognised us and chatted for a while and emphatically expressed that neither he nor his family had ever seen or heard anything out of the ordinary on that bridge or in the surrounding area.

About an hour later a police car pulled up and we spoke to the officers who informed us that one of the officers involved in the haunting was a P.C. Richard Ellis, and if I spoke to him personally, I would get a true accurate account of the haunting. Later that day I rang P.C. Ellis and arranged an interview with him. We arrived at Deepcar Police Station at about 7.pm and spoke to P.C. Ellis, who told us that he first heard of the haunting when two

Security guards, Steven Brooks and David Goldthorpe, from Constant Securities, Mexborough, had arrived at the police station in a highly agitated state to report seeing a phantom figure on Pearoyd Bridge in the early hours of the morning.

It was well after midnight that the apparitions had been seen, while they were on a routine patrol of the area. Intense darkness had engulfed the two men as they drove towards Pearoyd Bridge, when suddenly, in the brilliant glare of their headlights, a group of very young children appeared, playing around a pylon, as if performing some kind of ritual dance. Their laughter vibrated eerily through the still night air, before softly fading away, along with their tiny spectral images.

Although shaken by what they had seen, the two guards carried on with their work. But, a few nights later, as they were driving on Pearoyd Bridge, Steven stopped abruptly as the ghostly spectre of a man in a long black cloak and a cowled hood, appeared directly in front of them. Fear gnawed at their guts as they sat unable to move with shock, and then common sense prevailed.

Switching on the full headlights, Steven edged the vehicle closer to the apparition, and gasped in horror as the beam of light shone straight through the awesome figure.

Then, panic set in. He slammed his foot down hard on the accelerator and sped away from the terrifying sight.

It took a while for the men to regain their composure before they radioed through to their boss at Mexborough and told him what had happened. Mr Lee contacted the police to ask if they could help in any way as his men were scared half out of their minds, and dare not go back to the site. In the meantime the guards had also contacted the local vicar, Stewart Brindley, to ask for his help, but he declined and sent them to the police.

P.C.Ellis told the guards there was not much he could do, but they would look into the matter and put a report in if they found anything out there. The rest of the week was hectic, and as Saturday night came around, it was quiet in the police station. The officers were sat talking amongst themselves, waiting for any problems that may occur at any time. P.C. Ellis had been talking to Special Constable John Beet, about the haunting on Pearoyd Bridge, and as it was coming up to midnight and not too far from the time that the two security guards had seen the apparition, asked if he would like to go to the haunted site and take a look.

It was more out of curiosity than anything that P.C. Ellis wanted to go up there. Of course, the Special Constable was only too pleased to go. It was to be an experience to be remembered. They did not say anything to the other officers about where they were going, as they were likely to follow and pull a few pranks on them. So the two of them left as unobtrusively as they could, saying that they would call in later, and drove up to the site.

As the new by-pass road was not far from the police station at Deepcar, it did not take long to arrive at their destination near the bridge. Pearoyd Bridge used to cover a single road, but it was under construction to widen the span for the dual carriageway that was being excavated beneath it, turning the whole road into a blanket of slush and mud.

When P.C Ellis turned off the well-lit road and drove through the dark gully, the car spun as it hit the worst patches of really deep slush, and sank into the ruts where the excavators had been working. Luckily, he knew how to handle his car and within a short time he managed to reach the place where he wanted to be, facing the bridge.

He parked smack in the middle of the unconstructed road facing towards the bridge and the pylon, where the two suspected sightings had been reported.

He switched off all the lights, both in and outside of the car, and then the radios were turned off so that they could concentrate on any unusual sounds that they might hear. Above them the moon was bright and the stars twinkled against the inky darkness of the clear September night, while below, pitch blackness surrounded the two officers waiting in the haunted hollow.

Eventually, their eyes became accustomed to the dark and they found that they had a good view all around. They could see a good mile behind in the rear mirrors. To their right was a two hundred foot banking, a thirty foot banking lay to the left, and bang in front of them a hundred yards plus, was the haunted bridge.

There was no chance of anyone else sneaking up, as the whole area was caked in sludge, and both had the car windows down so they would hear if anyone was about. Nobody in their right mind would have tried walking about in that, even just to pull a prank.

As they sat waiting, P.C.Ellis noticed something moving around a large white stationary object up on the bridge and nudged the other officer, who had already seen it.

Both agreed there was a shadowy form moving from side to side of the white square and decided to go up and have a look. The ground was treacherous underfoot, but nevertheless they managed to make their way up the muddy banking and onto the bridge. But, on reaching the white object and searching the vicinity, they found nothing suspect and returned to the car.

In no time at all the shadow returned. "Right, that's it! Let's get back up there," P.C.Ellis said. "And this time, we take torches, but don't use it until we get to the top." Once more they climbed up the slushy banking and waited until they had reached the top before using the torches, but the shadowy form had gone. They scoured the whole of the bridge and the surrounding area, but there was nothing. After waiting in the darkness for a short while, they realised that nothing else was happening, so they scrambled back down the backing and got into the car. To be quite honest, they were relieved at not finding anything out there!

As it was a fairly warm night, P.C. Ellis had his arm resting on the window frame. Nothing had frightened them about the whole affair; to them it was just another incident to be investigated. But the phenomenon that was about to happen was identical for both officers, and it did unnerve them. Going from what had been a fairly relaxed atmosphere, they experienced a sudden feeling of intense cold. P.C.Ellis said, "It was as if someone had just walked over my grave." Shuddering, he drew back into his seat as tension filled the whole proximity about them and froze as paralysis set in, he could neither move a limb nor utter a sound.

It was abnormally cold as if being in a freezer. He had never experienced a coldness like it, and could not believe what was happening to him. Although his mind was working normally, no part of his body was responding to his rational thoughts. 'What the hell is happening here?' P.C.Ellis screamed inwardly. He knew some unseen being was watching them, it was too close, oppressively close for his liking, and fully understood that they were in grave danger.

His mind raced, 'How do I get out of this?' With a supreme effort, P.C Ellis managed to free himself from the horrific, crippling numbness that had engulfed him, and jerked his head stiffly from side to side. 'This is no good,' he said to himself. 'Come on, Richard, pull yourself together, you're frightening yourself.'

With great concentration, he effectively managed to calm himself as much as he could, and turned towards his partner, saying, "John, what the bloody hell's going on here?" The sound of his voice immediately broke through the force that was rendering John immobile. John let out a horrified scream and brought his arm around with a terrific force, landing a heavy blow across P.C.Ellis's throat, thoroughly winding him. At the same time he saw what John's gaze had been fixed upon.

Between the roof and the window frame was the torso of a man standing there. In the darkness they could not see any features on the figure hovering beside them, only that he was dressed in a paisley waistcoat and the rest of his clothing was entirely black. It seemed as if he had wanted them to see him before he slowly disappeared. John was in a bad state of shock, but by now P.C. Ellis had his wits about him.

His first thoughts were, 'we're being set up. It's some of the lads larking about. Somebody's going to catch it here!"

He grabbed his torch, leapt out of the car and ran around it, shining the beam everywhere. Although he could not see anything, he was still suspicious of the people he worked with as they were always pulling tricks on each other. Upon shining the light under the car, he realised that no one would be stupid enough to get under the car in all that filth and muck. It was then realisation dawned on him when he stopped and thought, 'this is weird, there are no footprints here except my own.' He went around to check on John's side of the car. There were only John's footprints leading from the car and back, going up the banking. If anyone else had been about, their footprints would have shown up also as he was standing in very deep slushy mud.

His flesh crawled. P.C.Ellis was not very happy with the situation and made a point of getting back into his car, and very quickly wound his window up and then locked himself in. John had now regained his composure and could talk about his fear. Both men had experienced the same events. The whole incident was completely inexplicable.

P.C.Ellis decided that it was time for reinforcements, but as he was parked in the dip he could not use the car phone, so he drove up onto Pearoyd Bridge and radioed through for extra men. He was told that they would be with him in a few moments. Breathing a sigh of relief at being out of the hollow they sat back to await their colleague's arrival.

Within seconds, a tremendously heavy thud landed on top of the car boot, causing the men to jump with fear.

"My god, what was that?" P.C.Ellis shouted, leaping from the car. John stayed put; he'd had enough with the last experience. Nothing was there.

Feeling apprehensive, P.C.Ellis got back into the vehicle and said to his colleague, "there is absolutely no way that anyone could have come up to the car and not been seen." The simple reason was that they had not been there long enough, and with the traffic lights on the bridge, they would have seen anyone else there. Before he could say another word, another thud hit the car. This time the noise was deafening and a freezing mist began to envelope them. The temperature began to drop swiftly.

"Bugger this," he yelled to his mate. I'm not staying here another minute longer, it's getting silly." Without a moment's hesitation, he started the car and drove away from the bizarre phenomenon, leaving it as far behind as possible.

When he met up with the other officers he told them of the happenings, and noted that the last lot had occurred at exactly 12.30. With reinforcements on hand, P.C. Ellis went back out to the haunted site, but he said, "not another damned thing happened."

A few days following the interview, I went out again to see P.C Ellis and we drove out to the haunted site together. By now, the road had been made up beneath the bridge so it was easier to walk about, and as it was yet to open to the public we knew we would not be disturbed by anyone.

The night was calm and clear, but after we had alighted

from his vehicle and proceeded to where the strange happenings had occurred, we noticed that even though it was not very late, the darkness had begun to settle abnormally fast about us.

Disturbing though it was, P.C.Ellis brushed it to one side and pointed out the locations of where he and Constable Beet had been parked on each occasion, and also pointed out where the guards had seen the apparitions.

As we were talking I sensed a change in atmosphere. The air was becoming oppressive and carried with it an overwhelming presence of evil. Aware of what could develop, and without saying a word to P.C.Ellis, I managed to steer him back to the vehicle, telling him that I would like to go back there on my own.

Leaving him standing by the Land Rover, I walked forward into the darkness to where I had felt the presence and tried to communicate with it, but all I could sense was a malevolent hatred that was trying to force me away from that particular area. Sadly, I had no choice but to join the officer, who had to admit that he was slightly afraid. I must admit that I had never come across such an intimidatory, sense of malicious evil that hovered beneath that bridge.

To be quite honest, we were both relieved to jump into the Land Rover and drive back through the bright welcoming urban lights to the safety of the police station.

P.C.Ellis admitted that he had been thoroughly shaken by the events that had occurred over the past weeks. He said, "After thirteen years in the police force, you have to be prepared for anything. It's alright, everyday occurrences, you can cope with that, but when you are dealing with a haunting, then it's a bit different."

Stocksbridge:
London Weekend Television Interview and the Phenomena that Followed

In June 1994, David Alpin and Maria Richmond from London Weekend Television rang to ask me if I would consent to be interviewed, and give my version as to what happened at Stocksbridge for the programme 'Strange but True.' I agreed, and was told that I would be informed of the date when it came closer to the time for filming.

Maria rang me on Sunday the 10th July to say that they would be filming at Stocksbridge on Thursday, the 14th, and could I be there at 2pm? I contacted an acquaintance, Leoni Sabetti, to ask if she would like to come out to the haunted site with me on the Wednesday, the day before filming, as the landscape had now been altered, and I wanted to find the exact location of where Leslie and I had been pushed, so that I could point it out to the film crew. Leoni agreed and we arranged to meet at my home on the following Wednesday morning.

Within a few short hours that same day, Leoni sprained her ankle – this injury was to have a significant connection as to what occurred later. Wednesday the 13th dawned and looked as if it was going to be a bright day.

I was very pleased for I knew that I would be able to investigate the area thoroughly, without being covered in sludge as I had been in the past. As we drove over the moors, I mentioned to Leoni that we would be driving past a stretch of woodland of an unusual character, that lay on the outskirts of Oughtibridge, a couple of miles before Stocksbridge. I had been informed, that on separate occasions, reliable people had witnessed mysterious balls of light darting at all angles and heights amongst the trees on the hillside. I had driven past this locality many times, but had never stopped. I suggested we take a look at the site before carrying on to Stocksbridge.

Knowing that there was a large parking area across the bridge to our left near a forge, I pulled in and parked close to the entrance so that if an emergency arose, I could make a speedy departure. Leoni checked the bandage around her swollen ankle before we set out on our walk. First of all we had to climb over a low stone wall, before scrambling up the steep embankment ahead into the wooded area, and didn't stop until we were on a more even patch of ground to regain our breath and contemplate our next move.

While we stood looking at the surrounding trees and bushes, we became conscious of the abnormal silence in the woods and apparent lack of wildlife. Usually there is the occasional nosy rabbit to be seen, but there was nothing. Not even one little bird could be heard singing or fluttering about in the trees. Over the years I have become accustomed to this kind of phenomenon, knowing that whenever there was a noticeable lack of wildlife, something malevolent was about, and mentioned this to Leoni. I also advised her to be on the look-out for any unusual sights or sounds.

No sooner had I spoken when she whispered, "Elisa,

someone is watching us." Instinctively, I bent down and pretended to be looking at something on the ground, and motioned Leoni to do the same, while at the same time I picked up a thick piece of broken tree branch, and pushed the other part towards her. The instant we straightened up and faced towards the direction of the intruder, we saw what looked like a very tall, thin man dressed in black, dart behind a bush and stay there.

Puzzled, but not deterred by this unusual action, and relieved that we were armed with our make-shift weapons, we carried on walking, regardless of the fact that we were very much aware that he was following.

A few moments later, however, we were surprised to catch sight of him at a slightly higher angle up the slope above us, where he suddenly dashed out from behind a tree, into some heavy shrub, before leaping out and hiding behind a bush. Something was amiss and I didn't like it. "What do you think we should do?" Leoni whispered. "I suggest we wait for a few minutes and watch to see what he does next. You can't be too careful." I replied.

We waited patiently for a while, but as nothing more occurred we decided to try and find out what the person was up to, and held our sticks at the ready, as we pushed our way through the undergrowth never taking our eyes from the bush where we had last seen him. There was no chance of him slipping past us without being seen, for the area surrounding the bush was unobstructed by any foliage.

As we approached the spot however, the temperature began to drop confirming our suspicions that this was no ordinary mortal we were dealing with. Taking a great deal of care and caution we carried our search and were not in the least bit surprised to find the bush deserted by the extraordinary person, but became concerned when the atmosphere began to change, for suddenly there was no air to breathe.

"Come on, we're getting out of this now," I said. I grabbed Leoni's arm, dragging her as I ran and did not slow down until we reached the wall from where we had started, only to stop dead when we saw the figure appear hovering beside the driver's door of my car. In unison with its appearance, the dog from the farm across the river began to howl mournfully and the geese created an horrendous racket.

Poor Leoni winced as she hobbled towards the car, then stopped and said, "eh, what if it comes with us? I'm not getting in the car if that thing's in it."

"Don't worry about that just now. The pentagram cover I have over the seat is there to protect us from anything like that happening," I told her.

Luckily, the being disappeared within seconds of our reaching the car, leaving us very relieved as we hurriedly jumped in, and without a moment's hesitation, sped away!

It only took fifteen minutes to reach Pearoyd Bridge at Stocksbridge, where I parked the car outside the farmer's entrance, in the exact spot that I had done a few years previously. I was pleased to find a new added attraction to the area; a picnic site where a wooden table with bench seats had been placed.

We were sickened, however, to find a trail of fresh blood,

spread along the centre of one of the bench seats, and could not imagine where it could possibly have come from as there were no birds flying over the site, and there never had been when I had visited the area before. There was no sign of any dead animal remains either, which was very puzzling.

We next walked onto Pearoyd Bridge and took photographs of the road and bridge, the motorway below and of each other, where Leslie and I had experienced the phenomenon of pushing and time loss. Leoni took the lower path, while I walked higher to try and find the exact position of where Leslie and I had been. We had walked about two hundred yards, when, simultaneously, we both looked and called to each other, and pointed to return from where we had started. By the time we reached each other we were both close to tears, and were astonished to find that we had, at the same time, begun to relive unhappy traumatic childhood memories.

Even though we felt the whole effect distressing, we did find it interesting, and agreed to return to the spot where I had been standing, as I had sensed the area of where the phenomenon had first started, when Leslie and I had heard the footsteps behind us, and proceeded warily forwards.

It was then that we spotted the insects. On certain blades of grass that were seeding, the lava of butterflies that had half-emerged from their chrysalis were all dead. It was a graveyard of nature. Even weirder was the fact that upon checking the measurement covered by the dead lava formed a perfect eight foot circle. That was enough proof for me. The place was still active, and we wanted no part of it, therefore we left.

We had used three cameras for filming that day, and each

roll of film developed came out blank. The next day, Thursday, the 14th, I met David Alpin, Maria Ridonat and the film crew from London Weekend Television at Stocksbridge to participate in the filming of 'Strange but True.' By now I hated the place and wished that I was safely back home. I knew something was amiss, but couldn't quite put my finger on it.

I should have realised when LWT arrived they wanted to film me in a completely different location to where we had experienced the phenomena, which was close to the picnic area where Leoni and I had seen the blood on the seat. I told them that we were in the wrong place but they would not listen and interviewed me there.

All the time I could feel a heavy sense of presence pushing at me, telling me to go away. Something did not want any of us there, and I was pleased when the interview was over so I could return home.

The following Friday we began to have a run of bad luck. Two of our workmen who were laying flags for a customer, fell and hurt their legs and ankles and could barely walk. My husband, who stayed at home, fell out of the back door, hurting his leg and knee. On Sunday, I fell and sprained my ankle. That night as I lay in bed, I knew that all of these injuries were no accident. Something from out at Stocksbridge was causing them. Incredibly, the moment the thought came to me, two loud bangs issued from the corner of my bedroom.

I sat up and switched on the bedside lamp, when to my amazement my bedroom door flew open and Leslie rushed in, but stopped suddenly and stared, pointing towards a figure draped in black standing by my bedroom window. "Good, god," I said, and leapt out of bed, but the thing disappeared before I could do anything.

"Oh, mum, what's happening?" Leslie cried, sitting on my bed. "I couldn't sleep because everything that had frightened me when I was little came at me in the darkness. My room was full of monsters, then I heard two loud bangs coming from your room, and then that horrible thing was standing there. Dad and I told you not go back to Stocksbridge, we knew something bad would happen, and so did you."

I had to admit she was right. We talked for a little while longer, and when her nerves had settled she went back to her own room. My husband, who has his own bedroom, slept through it all, and never heard a thing.

The following evening a friend of ours, Keith White, who is a joiner, rang to tell me that he had escaped death by inches. He had been working with his friend, John, removing old interwoven fencing in his garden, and as Keith was leant over swing a piece of timber, John had jumped onto the machine and was dragging at an awkward piece of fence, when suddenly a loose bracket shot off and flew through the air, straight down the neck of Keith's t-shirt, scoring a deep graze along his chest before emitting under his left arm pit, leaving a huge tear in his shirt.

Thoroughly shaken, Keith had stepped back and fallen, twisting his leg and ankle so badly he could not work for the rest of the week. His foot was still bruised and black when he called to see me the following week. Something strange had happened as he fell however; he saw me quite clearly and thought of Stocksbridge! This was no coincidence, for as the week progressed, friends and acquaintances were hurting themselves, and I was pleased when Leslie arrived home from Harrogate. We performed protective rituals for everyone concerned, and the accidents ceased.

Although Stocksbridge holds a fatal attraction for me, my family and friends have agreed that it is an area to be avoided at all times from now on!

P.C. Richard Ellis gave me an interesting selection of ghostly hauntings that have occurred in the Stocksbridge area.

The first one is of a monk who is reputed to haunt the old Underbank Hall. People who have worked and stayed overnight at the hall have heard mysterious tapping and movements that cannot be accounted for. A shadowy figure has often been seen gliding about the gardens, causing a weird sense of vulnerability to those who see it.

The second is of a ghost that took a dislike to the landlord after he began to cater for weddings at his public house. It made his life a misery by ruining the wedding preparations, and then moving heavy furniture about in his bedroom.

The third is of UFO phenomenon that was witnessed by hundreds of people in the Oughtibridge and Sheffield area.

The Monk

The monk was feeling very tired when he reached Underbank Hall after journeying from Lincolnshire, and was on his way to Alderman's Head. As he was so exhausted he called at the Hall and asked if they would oblige him with a night's lodgings. The owners agreed, but asked, if on the following day he would pay for his night's keep and food, by doing a day's work in the gardens. He was happy to do this, so he was given his supper and a place to wash and sleep.

The following morning after breakfast, he set to work with other men digging and weeding in the vast floral gardens. As he worked he listened to the songs of the birds as they flew from tree to tree. He breathed the fragrant perfumes that emitted from the exotic colourful blossoms about him. To him this was heaven on earth. He felt so at peace with nature there that he asked to be kept on. The owners agreed and he stayed.

As the years passed by and the monk became older, he asked that his last wish be granted; that after he died his body would be interred in sacred hallowed ground. It was not to be.

It is rumoured that his remains were buried in a little wood at Underbank Hall, where he had happily worked for so many years. It is in these woods and gardens that his apparition has been seen.

One day, while the gardeners were working on the lawns and flower beds, a dog from a nearby farm was taking its usual walk through the gardens, when it suddenly stopped. With its fur bristling, the animal crouched down low, snarling and growling, baring its teeth. Its eyes were fixed on a particular spot and it steadily backed away. The workmen could see nothing that could have disturbed the dog as it was out in the open, but the animal was aware of something before it. It carried on snarling and backing away for a few moments longer, then it rolled its eyes and ran away yelping. It never came back that way again.

P.C.Ellis could not find a record of any religious person ever having been buried in the local cemetery, so perhaps there is some truth then that the monk is buried at the Hall and the reason for him haunting, is that he is hoping that someone will come along and find his remains in order to replace them in consecrated grounds that he asked for!

The Ghost that didn't like Weddings

In 1976, the owner of The Star, a public house at Stocksbridge, experienced an aggressive, disrupting influence on the premises after he had started to cater for weddings.

Only hours away from the first wedding reception, the landlord found that the banquet, which had taken hours of careful preparation, was completely ruined and the room was in a shambles. Cooked foods, salads, cakes and trifles had been hurled with such force that they splattered all over the walls of the newly decorated room, and what had dropped to the floor had been trampled into the carpet.

Some of the food had large chunks bitten out of it, leaving teeth marks much larger than the average person's bite. Dismay flooded through him as he stared at the carnage before him, then gradually his shock turned to anger as he suspected that vandals had sneaked in and caused the damage.

This type of incident was to recur over and over again, even when the police were informed. They advised that all window and doors to the room be locked after the preparations were completed. But, as the wedding party arrived and the doors were unlocked, the room would be in chaos.

The problem was never to be solved and the police

remained baffled.

One night, as he laid in bed, the landlord was to undergo an alarming experience. Standing in the corner of his bedroom was a large Elizabethan wardrobe that he could clearly see in the semi-darkness. His mind boggled as he watched it slowly lift into the air and float across the room towards him. Letting out a yell he leapt clear as the huge object came crashing down on his bed. It was not until this happened that he fully realised that he was dealing with some kind of dangerous supernatural force.

On another occasion, while he was working in the bar one night, he and many of his customers heard a loud, heavy bang come from one of the upstairs bedrooms. They listened for a while but no other sounds came, so someone suggested they go up and have a look around, but the landlord said, "no, we might have burglars and they could be dangerous." He rang the police. The police arrived and within seconds took control of the situation, telling everyone to keep calm.

A search of the premises ensued, but nothing was found to be out of order, until they came to the landlord's bedroom, where they found something heavy was leant up against the door, and no matter how hard the officers pushed, they could not get into the room. The only solution was to go in through the bedroom window. A ladder was speedily brought and leant against the wall. The officer who went up was surprised to find that the window was fitted with a security lock, and he had to break in.

On gaining entry he stood for a few moments and surveyed the room before searching it, and was astonished to see the huge Elizabethan wardrobe standing directly in front of the door, barring it from anyone's entry or exit. It was weird. Without taking his eyes from it he backed up to the window and called for his colleagues to come up, and was relieved when the other officers climbed into the room and were standing beside him

Before moving the wardrobe they searched the bedroom, but no one else was there except them. They noticed that the carpet had not been disturbed and no other furniture moved. It took five policemen, all big burly chaps, to move the wardrobe back to its original place before anyone could get in or out of the room.

There was absolutely no way that anyone could have got out of that room with the big piece of furniture blocking the way, and no one could have got out of the window as it was locked from the inside.

Other landlords have taken the pub since, but as far as I am aware, no one else has experienced any form of psychic phenomena.

Was the wardrobe haunted?

UFO's Over Stocksbridge

The sighting came early one morning that heralded a bright sunny day in the beginning of the 1980's when a huge object appeared in the sky heading directly for Sheffield.

At the time, P.C.Ellis was working at Ecclesfield Police Station, and within seconds of the first sighting, the switchboard was blocked with calls from many frightened people. Staff who had been working on the night shift at the British Tissue works at Oughtibridge rang in to report the sighting, as did people from the Sheffield Steel works and the police from the Barnsley division, telling them to go out and see the spectacular, frightening monstrosity above them coming even closer.

P.C.Ellis went out with his colleagues and watched as the massive steel blue domed saucer came very slowly lower and lower until it was just hovering silently still, covering the whole area above. There was no sound coming from it, not were there any windows or lights. The thing was everywhere, one half of the sky was filled with it; the UFO was too big for anyone to comprehend. As they watched it, people said that it just looked as if the moon had come down from the heavens. As he and others talked, P.C.Ellis said, "You cannot put this down to mass hysteria; this thing is too damned big." It did not cast any shadow. The UFO stayed for a while longer and then swiftly and silently zoomed away.

Widely publicized was another UFO sighting in 1977-78, when hundreds of people rang the police to say that a large dog-bone shaped metal object was hovering in the sky on the north side of Sheffield. This stayed long enough for everyone to take a good look at it. The police have seen quite a few UFO's and things at night that cannot be explained.

Epilogue

During the interview with London Weekend Television I was asked by Maria Ridonat if I believed it was the monk haunting the new road at Stocksbridge, and the cause of the accidents. I told her no, I didn't think so.

With regard to the numerous traffic accidents on the A161 roadway, P.C.Ellis informed me that it had been suggested that the road is badly designed, and there is the possibility of a lack of good judgement by drivers using this stretch of road. It is a dark, twisting unlit road, and as it has a wide carriageway many people drive too fast.

I have driven along this road, and coming up to Pearoyd Bridge other vehicles headlights can cause imaginary figures, as they overtake on the opposite side of the road, especially when it is foggy.

With the publicity of ghosts it is possible that people are imagining that they are seeing these images.

I do not dispute what people say they have witnessed. I personally do not believe that it is the monk who is causing the accidents, as rumoured.

The monk is reputed to haunt Stocksbridge Hall and its gardens, and as he was a man of God and peace, then I find it in bad taste to suggest that he would injure or kill anyone.

As for the haunting on Pearoyd Bridge, it is possible that the construction company may have unwittingly disturbed the unmarked graves of the dead. With regard to the children dancing around the pylon; perhaps in the past, a maypole could have been placed there as part of the village celebrations for the children to dance around welcoming the sun coming up from the south (May Day), or, with it being close to a farming community, what better than a bonfire to celebrate the harvest gatherings, or even the Halloween festivities or a night to remember the dead. These are all our ancient customs, and these children could have been reliving them.

With retrospect to the man that the guards, Leslie and myself saw on Pearoyd Bridge, I am almost certain that it was John Dixon, the shotgun rider, protector of passengers and coaches, that was seen in the early hours of the morning waiting for the next coach to come along; all completely harmless apparitions.

A little over halfway down from the bridge to the new road, is a different complicated matter. This is the area where I was pushed with Leslie and lost time. It is also the place where I felt uncomfortable with P.C.Ellis and Leoni. The force was emanating down onto the A161 from that particular area. I am in complete agreement with what the Security guards said. There should be an exorcism performed at that bridge.

Perhaps if a full investigation of the area was carried out by a higher authority, and a blessing given for any disturbed souls there, then maybe the hauntings would cease.

P.C. Ellis

Lightning Source UK Ltd.
Milton Keynes UK
UKOW05f0732220813

215762UK00001B/3/P